5/00

AB

HIT IT RICH

Lee Packard and Hazel Manners wanted money, big money. More money than Packard could make as a small-time dip working the crowds around Oxford Street and Trafalgar Square. A bank robbery seemed just the thing, especially when the money had already been stolen and all they had to do was find it. It would have been easy but for the other people involved. These included Chief Superintendent Donald Martin of Scotland Yard, to whom the puzzle at first seemed to have no clues and no solution.

MICHAEL BARDSLEY

HIT IT RICH

Complete and Unabridged

LINFORD
Leicester

First published in Great Britain in 1972 by
Robert Hale Limited
London

First Linford Edition
published 2004
by arrangement with
Robert Hale Limited
London

British Library CIP Data

Bardsley, Michael
Hit it rich.—Large print ed.—
Linford mystery library
1. Detective and mystery stories
2. Large type books
I. Title
823.9'14 [F]

ISBN 1–84395–123–1

Gloucestershire
County Library

Published by
F. A. Thorpe (Publishing)
Anstey, Leicestershire

Set by Words & Graphics Ltd.
Anstey, Leicestershire
Printed and bound in Great Britain by
T. J. International Ltd., Padstow, Cornwall

This book is printed on acid-free paper

1

Terror came to Wiggin Street at ten-thirty on a warm spring morning.

That was the time when a grey Ford Zodiac, knocked off twenty minutes earlier near Willesden Junction station, pulled up outside the bank, its front end dipping as the driver applied the brakes violently. No one took any notice of it; everyone was busy hurrying about their own affairs. It was a Thursday, and the women were either shopping for the weekend or dragging reluctant children to the clinic which was about a hundred yards from the bank. The few men who were about were mostly workers from the nearby industrial estate, more concerned about their own problems than about anything which might be happening in the street.

Four men scrambled out of the car. The fifth stayed at the wheel; that could have been because the engine was still

1

running and he didn't want to fall foul of the traffic regulations, or there could have been some other, more sinister reason.

The men pushed through the crowds of people near the bank, moving swiftly and making it obvious that nothing was going to stop them. Once they were off the pavement and partially concealed in the lobby of the bank itself they stopped, two of them slipping knuckledusters over their fingers. Another produced a gun. The fourth slid a short crowbar from beneath his jacket.

They looked at each other, nodded, then pushed open the door of the bank and strode inside . . .

At eight-thirty that same morning, Chief Superintendent Donald Martin of New Scotland Yard had been woken by the shrilling of the telephone bell. The night before, he had stayed at his desk until nearly midnight, in an attempt to clear the paperwork which seemed to flood over it no matter what he did to try and stop it.

Endless reports to write and to read, facts to note, evidence to assemble, and all the time he was stuck inside other crimes were being committed which would need further reports, simply because men couldn't be sent to the scene quickly enough. The more men were tied up at desks, the more crimes were carried out which it might have been possible to prevent, and still more forms and typewritten statements were needed.

It was a vicious circle, and no one seemed able to do anything about it.

Now, he yawned, listening to the phone bell; for the moment it was in his mind to ignore it, as he had intended to sleep late that morning and go into the Yard about lunchtime, but then he slid out of bed and grabbed up the receiver.

His wife, Sandra, was already up, though the sound of the washing machine coming from the kitchen told him that she wouldn't want to be bothered with the phone.

'Martin,' he said curtly.

'Good morning, Don,' his assistant, Inspector Brady, said with sickening brightness. 'Sorry to disturb you. Did I get you out of bed or something?'

'You sound as if you hope you did,' Martin grunted. 'I hope this is something good.'

'Never can tell,' Brady said lightly. 'What I thought you might like to know is that there's a memo from Cranbourne just turned up on your desk. He's calling a special conference at nine-thirty.'

'Today?'

'That's right.' Brady still sounded too bright for that time of morning.

'It wasn't there when I left last night,' Martin said, sitting down on the edge of the bed and rubbing his eyes with his free hand. 'Where the hell's it been until now? This is a fine time to find it.'

'Search me,' Brady said. 'I just thought I'd better let you know about it.'

'Thanks very much. Next time, throw it away then at least I'll have a clear conscience when I say that I've never seen it.'

He rang off, yawned again and began to dress. There wasn't time for much breakfast, and by the time he hurried off to the Yard, still not properly awake, he was in no mood to sit in the office of the

4

Commander of the C.I.D. and discuss the rising crime rate and the best methods of fighting it. Some bitter remarks about time-wasting meetings were on the tip of his tongue, but he rephrased them into more diplomatic language before speaking, and wasn't surprised when most of the others agreed with him.

Even Commander Cranbourne, thin featured, white haired and wearing heavy rimmed spectacles, grinned and said that he might have a point.

Fortunately, the talking didn't go on for as long as he'd feared, mainly because some big shots were coming from Africa and Cranbourne was wanted to accompany the party as they were shown round.

'We'll have to stop there, gentlemen,' he said at five past eleven, glancing at his watch. 'I'd be glad if you'll think over what we've been saying, and if you've anything to add perhaps you'll pass them on to my assistant, Mr Hartle.'

There was a low muttering of voices as everyone stood up, followed by a scraping of chair legs, the tapping out of a pipe into an ashtray and the striking of a match.

'You're right, Don,' someone said to Martin. 'If there were more people actually policing and not acting as glorified filing clerks we could do a lot more than we're managing at present.'

Martin nodded, filing out of the office with the others, through the smaller room where Cranbourne's secretary was speaking in a low voice on the phone and into the corridor beyond.

'I know we're short of men,' he said, 'but that's not the whole answer. Only last week Johnny Swann was telling me that in his Division — '

He broke off as he heard a woman's voice calling after him, the sound cutting shrilly through the buzz of conversation.

He turned round.

'Could you spare another moment, Chief Superintendent?' Cranbourne's secretary said, smiling at him. 'The Commander wants to speak to you about a phone call which he's just received.'

'And what would you say if I told you that I was in a hurry?' he asked, following her back in to her office.

She didn't smile, but showed him into Cranbourne and closed the door.

Cranbourne was sitting at his desk, unusually grave faced, his spectacles on the desk in front of him. He waved Martin to a chair, and didn't speak for a moment.

'Trust this to happen when I've got this party coming round in five minutes,' he said eventually. 'I'm going to be late as it is.'

'What is it, sir?'

'A bank robbery,' Cranbourne said wearily. 'At a quick estimate fifty-five thousand pounds in small notes was stolen, but that isn't the worst of it. A passer-by who happened to get in the way of the thieves as they were leaving was hit over the head with a crowbar. Split his head open and killed him instantly . . . '

★   ★   ★

By the following morning the story of how Walter Deane had been murdered simply because he happened to get in someone's way was in every newspaper. Millions of people read it. Of those millions, hundreds of thousands were in London itself, and several of them were later going to be directly affected by the story, although they didn't yet know it.

One of them was a blonde named Georgina Lewis, who liked to read the paper every morning but who had got up late that day. As a result, she was reading it when she got to the office, where she was the sole employee apart from the boss. She had the paper spread out on her desk and was half-way down the column when a soft voice behind her made her jump and turn round, with a soft rustling of newspaper.

'I don't pay you to read the papers, Georgina,' her boss said. 'There are a lot of things which must be done today, even if you have to stay late.'

'Yes, Mr Cummins,' she said, and then smiled at him.

Some miles away, in a pokey flat, a model named Hazel Manners did her reading in far greater comfort than Georgina, sitting up in bed with a cup of tea on a table at the bedside. She skimmed through the story of the bank robbery, then turned quickly to the fashion pages, where there was a chance that her own photograph might look out at her.

An hour later, she had forgotten all about it, and she never mentioned it to her boyfriend, Lee Packard, when she saw him at lunchtime. It was left to him to find it out from his mates whom he saw in the pub; they were full of it, but their concern wasn't for the bank or the murdered man, but whether or not anyone they knew had been in the gang.

And at Scotland Yard, Donald Martin read every account. Each one seemed to make the crime more ugly than the last, but it was the photo of Deane's wife and three children in the *Echo* which really drove home how bad it was. So far there was no lead, either. The stolen car had been abandoned a few miles this side of Watford, and of the money that had been stolen the only notes that could be identified were five ten-pound notes; all the rest was in ones, and no one had any idea what their numbers were.

A week passed, then another and another and eventually a month.

Under Martin's guidance the police probed and questioned and checked, but still nothing came to light. After a day or two the newspapers dropped the story, though the *Echo* revived it after four weeks, asking why nothing had been done to find the killer of a man who hadn't been involved with the bank or the money or the robbery in any way, but had chosen that moment to walk past and get in the way of one of the men. Cranbourne asked the same question, too, though he already knew the answer; men were working constantly, but with nothing to guide them and little hope now of turning up anything new, there wasn't a thing they could do.

So the case closed up, and it was Hazel Manners' boyfriend, Lee Packard, in a private terror of his own, who caused the first cracks to appear in the solid wall.

2

Lee Packard ran.

His feet pounded along the pavement, his breath came in whistling gasps and his eyes were wide and staring, an indication of the terror he felt. He turned a corner of the dark street, ran a short way along another one, and turned a second corner. It was even darker here, for he was off the main road now and there were no street lights, but he still didn't slow down until he was halfway along it.

His chest was aching. He tried to draw air into his lungs, and thought that he'd never manage it, the pain was so great. Finally he took a couple of shuddering breaths, then looked back the way he'd come. The effort of running so fast had almost finished him off, causing his eyes to water and the two men who were chasing him look like four. The first time he'd seen that he'd blinked after staring hard, and the four images had gone back to two, but even two to one were impossible odds as far as Packard was concerned.

He was a short, snub-nosed man, but chunkily made. His fingers were the oddest part of him; in complete contrast to the rest of his body they were long and slim and so flexible that they could have been five snakes fastened to each hand. They were the most precious thing that Packard possessed, and he had actually insured his hands for five thousand pounds each.

It didn't cost him much to do it, and it was something that set him apart from the other pickpockets and petty thieves with whom he mixed.

'Got to cover the assets of the business,' he'd told Hazel Manners, not long after meeting her. 'Wouldn't do to have an accident with them and find that I couldn't work the dip racket no more, would it?'

She hadn't realized he was joking until he winked.

'Do you think they'll pay out?' she'd asked scornfully. 'What did you tell them you were to make your hands so valuable?'

'Told them I played the piano and organ in a few clubs, and I had to look after my fans. They'd better pay out if I ever have to make a claim.'

'And you'll take them to court if they don't, I suppose?'

They'd both laughed at that.

Packard wasn't laughing now.

He had no idea why the two men were following him, or what they wanted. They were both bigger than he was; if they caught him there was no telling what they might do. So far, they hadn't tried to catch him, though, but simply tagged along behind him wherever he went. He'd noticed them for the first time that night, when he'd left his flat. They'd followed him to the Marigold Club, and one of them had stayed near him all the time he'd been in there. When he'd left they'd split up, taking it in turns to keep behind him, presumably because they thought they'd be less noticeable that way.

Gradually, they'd seemed to close in on him.

It was a terrifying feeling, made worse because there was nothing he could do to stop them. He didn't know what they were after or why they'd picked on him; all he could do was try to lose them, and even that wouldn't be more than a temporary help because they knew where he lived and could easily pick him up again. Anything was better than the constant padding of footsteps behind him, though, even if it was only a break of a few hours.

Besides, if he could get rid of them for a while he might stand more chance of finding out what they were up to.

They were at the end of the street now, both of them, staring after him. One wore a long overcoat and cloth cap as he slouched along the pavement, looking like any old rag-bag of a tramp. The other was younger, taller, and was the one who'd come into the Marigold Club; there was nothing really outstanding about him apart from his blue eyes which glittered like a couple of gems whenever the light fell on them. No matter where Packard had gone in the club this man had been nearby. On one occasion, Packard had nearly spoken to him, but at the last minute he'd decided that it could mean trouble and had kept his mouth shut.

Turning down this street might have been the wrong thing to do, because it didn't lead anywhere except a scrapyard run by a fat slob called Johnny Spooner, and if the men had been wanting to trap him for some reason they could easily do it now, but that might be better than being trapped at his flat, with no chance at all of getting away, and nowhere to run to if he did.

That was the worst thing. There was nowhere at all he could go to for safety, no one who would give him help. If he did anything he'd have to do it on his own, and with two of them involved any plan would have to be pretty cute, and neatly carried out.

He hadn't hurried until he was round the corner, then he'd sprinted as fast as he could for a few yards, trying to get out of range of the street lamps on the main road before the men could turn the corner.

He was still breathing deeply by the time he stopped, near the wooden fence of the scrapyard.

Leading them back to his flat wasn't going to get him anywhere. The best thing as far as he could see would be to try and lead them into a trap, and get them apart. It would be risky, but once he could get the slouching man on his own he would probably be able to beat out of him what it was they were after. There was still a lingering fear in his mind that they were coppers, though with everything they did that possibility became more and more absurd. Cops had an air about them which stayed there all the time, even off duty. A stolid manner of walking. A way of looking at you as if they owned the world and everything in it.

These men weren't like that; they were more like mobsters, and the fact that a couple of jerks who could run with one of the big gangs were following him around made little shivers run up and down Packard's spine.

He turned, leaning on the scrapyard fence. Dimly in the darkness he saw the man with the glittering eyes at the other end of the street, peering forward, obviously unable to see anything.

His mate seemed to have vanished, but Packard didn't see anything significant about that.

He whistled softly.

The man's head jerked up and he began to walk slowly down the street towards him. Packard swallowed. Guns and knives weren't things that he normally had any use for as he worked the crowds at the Tower and in Oxford Street, and only now did it occur to him that this pair could be armed. If they were, they'd be able to pick him off any time they wanted, and he had made the biggest mistake of his life bringing them down here.

His breath rattled between his teeth.

If it was a mistake, it would be the last one he was ever going to make.

When he judged that the man was near enough to see him clearly he jumped up lightly and caught hold of the top of the fence. As quickly as he could he pulled himself over, then dropped on to the other side. Some bits of rusting metal got in the way and he nearly fell on them; at the last minute he managed to roll away and they rattled as his foot caught against them.

Without stopping he straightened up and ran across the open ground to an old car which loomed up as a black shape in the gloom.

As he turned to look back at the fence he saw the man with the glittering eyes scrambling over it. For a moment he was outlined against the sky, then he dropped down and vanished from sight. Hardly breathing, Packard waited behind the car, wishing that there was a little more light so that he could see what he was doing.

A faint sound came to his ears. The man was walking slowly, picking his way over the uneven ground and heading towards the car where Packard was hiding. He held his breath and listened, trying to decide exactly where the man was; it wasn't easy but he worked out that he would pass a good few yards to one side of the old car.

Suddenly he stopped.

There was no noise at all now, apart from that of a motorbike gathering speed along the main road, its engine clattering harshly in the still night air. The skin on the back of Packard's neck began to crawl as he crouched behind the wrecked car, knowing that the man was there yet unable to see him, unable to do anything other than wait for him to make a move so that he could guess where he was.

The noise of the motorbike faded away.

Out of the darkness came a whistle, something like the one Packard had used before.

It came from the other side of the scrapyard, and even with the noise of that motorbike to cover any noise he might have made, the man he'd seen climbing over the fence couldn't have got round there so quickly, not in the darkness and with piles of scrap to pick his way over.

So both of them were in the scrapyard now. The other one must have come in from the other side, hoping to cut him off before he could find anywhere to hide. He grinned savagely, realizing that they were better organized than he'd thought, then crept round to where he could look over the bonnet of the car.

He stared into the darkness on either side, but he could see no one. There hadn't been an answer to that whistle either, so the man with the glittering eyes must have realized that they were giving their position away by signalling. To help things along and to try and produce some action which would ease the strain on his taut nerves, Packard whistled himself, and was rewarded with an answer from the newcomer, the slouching man. Faint sounds came out of the night as someone began to creep cautiously towards the car.

Gently, Packard tried the door handle. It was very stiff, and when he pressed it down the door began to swing open slowly, creaking faintly.

He stopped.

Everyone else had stopped too.

This time the creeping sounds didn't start up again and there was still a complete silence. Packard was starting to think that maybe this was a lousy idea after all when a voice said softly:

'We know you're there Packard, so

don't try anything smart. It wouldn't be worth your while, and you'd only get hurt.'

He stayed very still, hardly breathing, holding the door to stop it from groaning.

There was a sudden stab of flame and the bark of a shot. He never felt the bullet nor heard it strike anything and it was obvious that it hadn't come anywhere near him. That didn't prove a thing but he reckoned that if they'd really wanted to kill him they could have done it before this, and it wouldn't have needed two men. The shot was more in the nature of a warning of what would happen if he didn't tell them where he was.

He did nothing except crouch behind the old car, trembling slightly.

'Don't push your luck,' the same voice said. 'I know you're there somewhere. You'd better come out now or the next bullet will be nearer.'

It was the word 'somewhere' which gave Packard the tip off that the man didn't really know where he was hiding. His eyes were getting used to the darkness now, and as he had been talking it had been easier than he'd thought to work out where the man must be. By straining his eyes in that direction he could make him out, a bulky shape against the dark sky, very still and his arm partly raised as he held the gun.

Packard's groping fingers found a stone; he picked it up and tossed it lightly towards the man, who whirled when it hit the ground with a rattling noise.

At the same moment Packard slammed the car door shut then ran across the lumpy ground, towards a hut which he knew wasn't far away. The gun barked again, and a voice said sharply.

'Quit that shooting!'

It was much nearer than Packard had expected and he almost stopped running. There was no one in sight, though, and he reached the hut, which served as an office for Johnny Spooner. As he'd expected, the door was locked, but he wasn't really bothered about getting in; he was more concerned with trying to bewilder the two men, to get them running about the yard until they didn't know what they were doing, then pounce and grab one of them.

A shadowy figure walked past about ten yards away. It was the slouching man, but he wasn't slouching now. The cloth cap had gone and he was standing straight, making him much taller than Packard had realized. His movements were brisker too, and Packard broke into a sweat as he saw that things weren't going to be as easy as he'd thought. The man turned. Packard tried to dodge back out of sight, moved clumsily, and caught his foot against the side of the hut. He didn't think anyone had heard it but to his alarm there was a sudden shout.

'Come on, Terry, over here.'

There was nowhere he could go to get away from them. The hut was almost against the fence, with only a space of a foot or so between them, but if he tried to climb over he was certain to be spotted. He crouched back and saw Terry, the slouching man, hurrying over, his body just a featureless lump in the darkness.

'Where is he, Mark?' Terry breathed.

'Somewhere near this shed,' Mark said. 'You go round that way.'

They split up and Packard heard the soft noises as they crept along. He squeezed himself between the hut and the fence as hurriedly as he could. Being trapped like this wasn't what he had had in mind when he'd come in here but unless he could break past one of them at the corner of the hut there was no way in which he could avoid being caught. He waited, almost groaning aloud, and heard Mark coming slowly alongside the hut, his arm making a scraping sound as it brushed against the wood.

He reached the corner.

Before turning it, he stopped.

Packard saw him and lashed out, catching him in the face and sending him staggering back. As he jumped forward there was a confused sound behind him and an arm came grabbing out of nowhere. He turned swiftly, hitting out at this new threat, but before he could deal with it Mark had recovered his balance and was coming up.

He had a gun in his hand and he was grinning.

3

'Got him, Terry?' he demanded.

Terry grunted and pushed Packard against the wall. He didn't get hold of him again, but with the gun almost touching his chest it wasn't worth trying to make a break for it; before he'd gone two yards he'd be dead, or at least injured. Instead, he leaned easily against the hut, trying to give the impression that he couldn't have cared less what they wanted, and looking from one to the other of them.

They were an odd pair, Mark smart in his short coat and the suit he had worn in the Marigold Club, and Terry still in the scuffy raincoat he had worn in his role as the slouching man. The thing that most terrified Packard now was the way they were looking at him, both with flat, expressionless, snake-like eyes and mouths that were set in a straight line; they gave the impression that they didn't regard him as a human being but as something to be used until they'd got what they wanted and then destroyed.

He shivered slightly.

'Well?' Terry asked, with a grin in which there was no humour at all.

'You disguise yourself pretty well,' Packard said. 'You make yourself too noticeable, that's all.'

'What do you mean?' Terry's eyes narrowed and he stared at Packard as if he was wondering why he wasn't frightened.

'When I first saw you I thought you were a tramp. A little later on I spotted you again. Someone who really slouched along like that all the time would never have been able to keep up with me.'

'Smart, aren't you?'

'Skip it,' Packard said. 'What do you want?'

'You know what we want,' Mark said, jabbing him with the gun. 'Where's the girl?'

'Which girl?' Thoughts of Hazel Manners came into Packard's mind, and he shuddered at the possibility that she might be tangled up with characters like these.

'Don't be clever,' Terry said. 'You thought you were smart coming in here, didn't you, but you'll soon find out what a punk trick it was.'

Packard took a breath. Where they were standing was right at the back of the yard, about as far away from the main road as they could get. There was a road just the other side of the fence, but it was only a side street and there was little chance of anyone coming along it at this time of night. Running in here and getting caught was probably the worst thing that could have happened, but there was no time to worry about it now.

'Where is she?' Terry insisted, while Mark gave him another savage jab with the gun.

He could tell them the truth and say that he didn't know what they were talking about. If he talked persuasively enough he could probably convince them that they'd made a mistake, but the most likely outcome of that would be a bullet through the head as soon as they were certain he was telling the truth. The other way was to make them think they were right, keep them talking until they were offguard, and try to get away from them.

Though as they knew where he lived that wouldn't get them off his back.

There seemed no way out.

While he was standing working things out Terry reached casually into his pocket. He brought out a gun much like Mark's and grinned.

'Stop jabbing me with that gun,' Packard said, his voice made sharper by the knowledge of his own helplessness.

'We'll jab you with a bullet in the teeth in a minute,' Terry said, giving him another vicious poke.

'Listen, Packard,' Mark said, 'you're only playing for time. We know you've got Georgina Lewis hidden away. All you've got to do is tell us where she is and we'll quit bothering you. That's a fair bargain, isn't it?'

'Suppose I don't tell you?'

'Then it's a bullet in the brain.'

'It's your choice,' Terry told him, backing up Mark. 'Where is she, Packard?

Are you going to tell us or shall we shoot you?'

Packard ran his tongue over his lips. He looked from Mark to Terry and back again. Their faces were indistinct in the darkness but he could see enough to tell him that there was no hope in either of them. Shooting him wouldn't put them in any danger; when the cops found his body there would be nothing to connect him with Mark and Terry, no reason for them to fear an investigation. They would simply fade away and things would go on much as before.

Except for him.

And maybe Georgina.

Had he known who she was and where she was hiding he might have told them. As he'd never heard of her he couldn't do a thing. He couldn't even tell them he didn't know who she was because at the end of it, when he convinced them that they'd made a mistake, they'd shoot him just the same.

'Come on, Packard, snap it up,' Mark said.

'If I don't tell you, you'll shoot me?' he

asked, playing for time, desperately trying to think of a way out of the mess.

'That's right.'

'Then you'll never find out where she is,' Packard said. 'That wouldn't be so smart, would it?'

'Listen, Packard,' Mark said, 'we know you've got Georgina. We aren't guessing at it.'

'So?'

'She isn't at your flat. All we want to know is where you've hidden her. She doesn't mean so much to you that you'd let us kill you rather than say where she is, does she?'

'What about Hazel?' Terry sneered. 'She wouldn't like it if you thought so much about another bird, would she?'

Fresh alarm stabbed through Packard.

'What do you know about Hazel? Have you — '

'We've done nothing yet. What we might do depends on how fast you talk.'

Packard shook his head slowly.

'It won't work,' he said. 'I don't trust you. You'll have to be a lot more convincing than that if you want me to tell you anything.'

He knew that while he was talking like this he was as good as admitting that he knew where the girl was, but he couldn't see any other way of keeping himself alive. All he wanted was some diversion which would take the hard stare off him for a moment; it was easy enough to think that, but to try to cause one, even, might result in a bullet.

The two men exchanged glances.

It wasn't much but for a moment that was almost too brief to be of any use to him neither of them was looking at him. His right elbow smashed into Mark's stomach and at the same time he knocked the gun upwards. It went off as he hit Terry in the teeth, forcing the other gun aside, and the sound of the shot being fired so close to his ear almost split his head open.

Mark was recovering quickly. Packard hooked his legs from under him and saw the gun flick out of his hands and spiral away into the darkness. Quickly, he ran across the yard, away from the hut and towards the part of the fence where he had climbed over. The darkness swallowed him up quickly and he reckoned he was safe from a bullet for the moment, as he concentrated on getting past the heaps of scrap without falling and breaking his neck he knew that the main danger would come when he tried to climb over the fence.

He thought he stood a good chance of getting away.

Not that it would do him much good if he did, for they would come after him to his flat, but at least it would get him out of the terrifying surroundings of the scrapyard. It had been stupid to come here. He could see that now as he tripped and nearly sprawled on the ground in his haste.

He reached the fence and stopped running. For a moment he thought that the crack of the gun-shot must have caused some damage inside his head, because the sound of running feet went on while he was standing still, but then he realized that one of the two men must be very close.

The laboured thumping of his heart

almost drowned the noise of the foot-steps. His fear was so great that it seemed as though he could hardly breathe. No one was in sight, but that was nothing to go by and after a moment's dangerous indecision he jumped hurriedly for the top of the fence.

Too hurriedly. His grip slipped off, his fingers rasped painfully against the rough wood, and he was unable to choke back a faint grunt as he hit the ground. By the time he'd scrambled to his feet he knew that it was too late for a second try, and turned to face Terry.

He was coming towards him, crouch-ing, his eyes glittering like Mark's telling Packard that there was no hope now. If they caught him this time they wouldn't stand talking; they'd simply beat him to pulp until he told them where the girl was, and then kill him.

'Now look — ' he began, the words bubbling out of his mouth in his terror.

Terry came nearer.

Packard hit out.

Terry laughed softly, stepped back out of reach then came in swiftly, weaving from side to side. Packard hit at him again and again, but found every time that he wasn't quite where he'd expected. Suddenly a fist flicked out and caught him on the side of the head. There was more power in it than he'd have thought possible, and he was sent staggering against the fence.

Terry took the gun out of his pocket again and jabbed him savagely with it.

'Where is she, Packard?' he demanded.

Packard shook his head, apparently dazed. He staggered forward then lunged suddenly, taking Terry by surprise. He grabbed for the gun, caught Terry's wrist instead, and began to bend his arm upwards. Terry grunted something unintelligible and Packard kicked at his ankles. He stumbled and his arm was forced a little farther back.

Packard's teeth ground together with the strain of trying to stop this powerful man bringing the gun down to point at him. If only he could wrench it out of his grasp they would be equal. His hand was slippery with sweat in spite of the coldness of the night air, and he could hear Terry gasping for breath, panting in his ear like a dog after a cat.

Where was Mark?

That was the important question. If he came to help there could be no hope, but if he kept away for another few minutes there was a faint chance that he would be able to win. What happened after that could be dealt with later.

He thrust at Terry's arm again. His fingers slipped over Terry's and he felt where they were curled round the trigger. Terry grunted. His arm was jerked upwards under the force of the push and the gun pointed straight at his head. At the same moment, he slipped. The sound of the shot as his finger tightened suddenly on the trigger almost deafened Packard, but it didn't prevent him from seeing the small hole which appeared in Terry's forehead.

4

As Packard stood in the darkness, staring down in a panic at the dead man, he realized that someone was shouting. With an effort he dragged his eyes away from the body and strained to see across the dark scrapyard. Mark. That was the worry now. He was the only other person around and if he came there would still be no escape.

The hoarse cry came again.

'Terry!'

Packard's brain began to work again, slowly at first. He realized from Mark's tone of voice that something was wrong with him and moved away from the body as quickly as he could, stopping when his arm touched the wooden fence.

'What's the matter?' he shouted, doing his best to imitate Terry's flat, clipped voice.

'I've fallen over some bricks!' Mark

cried thinly. 'What have you done with that punk?'

'He's taken care of.'

'Then for God's sake come and help me!' Mark shouted. 'I think I've broken my leg.'

Packard grinned into the darkness, now that the immediate panic was over and something of his normal calmness was coming back. He didn't mind being chased by two thugs, provided one was dead and the other had a broken leg; those were the sort of odds he could handle.

'Hang on!' he shouted, still trying to imitate Terry's voice. 'I'm coming. Stay where you are until I get there.'

He didn't wait to hear the answer to that but grinned again as a stream of curses started. Now that there was no hurry he didn't have much difficulty in getting over the fence and once he'd dropped down on the other side he began to breathe more easily. His clothes were splashed with mud and dirt; he wiped them as best he could, then hurried to the main road. Fortunately it wasn't far from here to his flat, so he wouldn't be in much danger of meeting anyone.

He looked at his watch.

There was mud on the glass but when he rubbed it off he saw that it was almost half-past one. Late, but not as late as he'd thought.

Terry had been killed. That was the thought which drummed in his brain as he hurried back to his flat. Apart from Mark there had been no witnesses and the only fingerprints on the gun would be those of Terry himself. No one could pin it on Packard and even if he went to the cops he could say it had been self-defence.

Could he?

Who would believe him?

From his experience of cops they believed no one without making a full enquiry and that was the last thing Packard wanted. Any enquiry into his affairs could do him nothing but harm, so it looked as though the cops were out on that score alone. In any event, squealing to the cops wasn't one of Packard's habits. Whatever the outcome of this was, whichever way they turned, he'd handle it alone; like that, there wouldn't be any slip ups caused by trusting anyone else.

Except Hazel.

He could trust her and he'd have to tell her, if only because she might have some idea who Georgina Lewis was. She was the one they needed to find; once that was done he'd have a better chance of taking Mark off his back.

He met no one on his way to the flat. By the time he reached it he was trembling from reaction to the shooting, and all he wanted was a glass of whisky in bed, then a good sleep until morning.

He walked up the short drive, went through the hall, up the stairs and along a short passage, his feet clumping on the bare boards. His flat was one of two on this floor of the converted house but he knew from experience that the other tenant wouldn't worry about the noise. Slipping his key into the lock, he opened the door and went in.

There was no hall, and the bedroom and bathroom were just parts of the main room which had been blocked off with hardboard partitions. He switched on the light, then stopped with his hand still on the surround of the switch, thinking that he had heard a faint sound.

Slowly, he lowered his hand, closed the door carefully, then stood very still, listening.

The sound, if it had ever been there, had gone.

Frowning, he walked to the middle of the room then worked his way stealthily towards the wall so that he'd be able to get a good look inside the bedroom from as far away as possible. He was very much aware that Mark and Terry knew where he lived, and there was a chance that more than the pair of them were involved, and the rest of the gang were waiting here for him to come back.

He reached the wall. From here he only had to move a couple of feet and he would be able to see most of the bedroom.

He took a short pace forward and then another, until he could see into the room.

There was no question of anyone hiding. The blonde who was in the bed was too frightened to worry about things like that. Packard swallowed then took another step forward, still cautious. The girl ran the tip of her tongue over her lips, then she said:

'Are you Mr Packard?'

He nodded, at a loss for something to say.

'Hi,' she said and smiled. 'I'm Georgina Lewis.'

5

Packard hesitated for a minute in the doorway. His head was throbbing, he was still in a mild state of shock after what had happened in the scrapyard, and all he wanted to do was go to sleep. At any other time the sight of a strange blonde in his bed would have excited him; now, it merely confused and irritated him. If Mark had arrived he would probably have told him to take her and get the hell away from him, leaving any questions and problems to be sorted out in the morning.

But Mark wasn't here.

'So you're Georgina Lewis, are you?' he said, going right into the bedroom, not certain what was the best thing to do. 'And what are you doing here?'

Like the rest of the house, and flat, the bedroom was nothing special, though he tried to keep it clean and tidy, and once a month he persuaded Hazel to give it a good going over. Apart from the times she was here, Georgina Lewis gave this room more class than it had had for years. He stared at her with more interest now that he could see her better. Most of her was still hidden underneath the bedclothes but as she struggled into a sitting position he saw that the rest of her figure was going to live up to the promise of her face.

She was wearing a white slip. A green top coat and a powder blue woollen dress were flung over the back of a chair, and a pair of shiny black shoes with big, clumpy heels were under it. She was still blinking in the glare of the light, as if she had been asleep, but there was a smile on her face.

She looked as if she was welcoming him home.

'What's the play now?' Packard asked, his voice slightly more cheerful than it had been.

She frowned at him.

'Do I get right in there with you?' His grin broadened. 'Or are you going to get up so I can go to sleep?'

The smile faded from her face slowly,

and she shook her head. Her blonde hair was tousled from the pillow and she patted at it with her fingers, trying to get it back into its proper style.

'I'll get up,' she said. 'Would you mind going into the other room while I put my dress on?'

'No fear,' he said. 'That's one of the risks you took when you broke in here. Nothing personal, but I'm staying where I can see you. I don't trust people who break in.'

Especially, he thought, when they're connected with people like Terry and Mark.

She flushed, then pushed the bed-clothes right back and swung her legs over the side.

'That's a mean thing to say. I don't know what I'm doing here, anyway.'

'Lady,' Packard said, looking her over, 'if you don't know, that makes two of us.'

She smiled. She was really something to look at, even when she wasn't smiling. She didn't make any comment on what he'd just said but picked up the woollen dress and pulled it over her head. After smoothing it over her hips she poked her hair again then turned to him.

'Is there any chance of a drink of something? Tea, if you've got it.'

'Make yourself at home,' he told her. 'Feel free to. There's no need to explain what you're doing here.'

'You make the tea and then I'll tell you what I'm doing here,' she said.

'Mark and Terry wouldn't treat you like this,' he told her as he turned away. 'They'd soon knock it into you that you can't always have your own way.'

'Mark and Terry?' she demanded, a sudden gleam of alarm coming into her eyes. 'What do you know about them?' She flopped down on the bed and stared up at him, bouncing up and down slightly as the springs gave beneath her weight.

'I've met them,' he said cautiously, 'but I don't even know their full names.'

'Mark Edwards and Terry Stevenson,' she answered promptly.

'And who are they? Why are they after you?'

'They aren't going to come here, are they?' she said, anxiety in her voice.

'I hope not. I've had enough for one night.' He was still standing near the entrance to the room. 'What I really want to do is go to bed. It's nearly two o'clock in the morning.'

'Have you a spare room?' Georgina said.

'Does it look like there's a spare room?' he asked, going back into the living-room and filling the kettle from the tap in the small alcove which served as a kitchen. 'I'm not rich enough to afford things like that.'

'If there was one I could sleep in there,' she said.

'Why not sleep at your own flat?' he asked, making it sound as if it was a novel suggestion. 'Or do you find it cheaper to live this way, flitting round from one place to another at other people's expense?'

He was laying out a couple of cups and saucers as he said that. A few moments later the kettle boiled and Georgina switched it off, taking over from him. She didn't speak again until the tea was made and they were sitting on the battered settee.

'What are you doing here?' Packard demanded, sipping the hot tea. 'I take it that you're on the run from Edwards and Stevenson, but why come to me? And who are they, anyway?'

'They want to kill me.'

There was so much lack of emotion in her voice that at first he didn't realize the full significance of what she had said. When it eventually got through to him he held the cup half-way to his mouth and stared at her.

'Kill you?'

She nodded.

He set down the cup and saucer.

'Why?'

She smiled faintly, shaking her head.

'That's the thing I don't know,' she told him. 'If I did I might be able to do something about it instead of just running away all the time.'

'How long have they been after you?'

'About a week.'

'And why didn't you come here when they first started? Why turn up now?'

She took another drink of the tea. Packard noticed that her hands were trembling, setting up a gentle clatter between the cup and the saucer, though he himself seemed to have become strangely calm. Perhaps it was the tea, though it was the first time he'd noticed it having that effect on him.

It was the first time he'd killed anyone, too. Perhaps that had something to do with it.

'I can't stay at my own place,' Georgina said, 'because they know where that is. I've been staying with a friend of mine but it didn't take them long to find out about that, so I had to go to another friend. Her name is Hazel Manners and she put me on to you.'

'As a home for distressed young ladies?' he sneered. 'How did you get in?'

'It wasn't very hard. Not when you know how.'

'And do you know how?' he asked her, his eyes narrowing.

'It's one of the things you pick up,' she said defensively. 'You, of all people, ought to know that.'

Packard's unease deepened. Just what had Hazel told this girl about him? He couldn't really see her shooting off her mouth to that extent, because she was too careful, but Georgina definitely seemed to know more than was good for her.

'Sure,' he said, 'I know that, but you must have picked it up pretty well because I didn't see any marks round the lock and there was no trouble getting the key in. It takes skill to open the door without damaging the lock.'

'It isn't the best lock in the world, is it? You can hardly compare it with the Bank of England, or somewhere like that.'

'Maybe not,' he said with a shrug. 'When I saw Edwards and Stevenson they were on their way here. Have you told anyone other than Hazel that you were coming?'

She shook her head.

He stood up and crossed to the phone, dialling Hazel's number quickly. There was no answer, and after a couple of minutes he had to hang up.

'I'll try her again in the morning,' he said with a worried frown. 'She must still be out somewhere, though I'd have thought she'd be home by now.'

'She was just leaving to go on a modelling job when I got to her flat,' Georgina volunteered. 'That was why she sent me to you. She said that you were a private detective and that you might be able to help me. I don't know how much it would cost but if it isn't too much I'll be able to pay you, so don't worry about that.'

Packard nodded absently. The idea of Hazel persuading this bird that he was a private detective amused him, and explained that earlier remark about the lock, but he couldn't see what reason she could have for doing it. The best thing would be to leave it till morning, when he would be fresher and when he could see Hazel and find out what she was considering. Things might have been altered by the fact that Terry Stevenson was now dead, but that was one of the things they could worry about later.

'How about the cops?' he asked suddenly. 'Why haven't you gone to them?'

That was important; if she was likely to want to run to the cops he wasn't having anything to do with her.

'The cops aren't friends of mine,' she said, in an unexpectedly hard voice. 'Don't mention them. I won't be running to them whatever happens.'

He nodded and yawned. It was coming up to half-past two in the morning, and after all he'd been through he was feeling ready to pack it in for a few hours.

'I'll see what I can do with the case in the morning,' he said, trying to sound like a private detective. 'In the meantime I'd better get some sleep. It looks as though I'm going to finish up on the settee.'

She shook her head.

'It's you who's going to have to do the work,' she said at once, 'and it's your bed after all. I'd like to stay here all day tomorrow, so if I'm tired I can always have a sleep while you're out.'

He wasn't in the mood to argue with her. Fifteen minutes later he was in bed and asleep, troubled only by a dream in which Terry Stevenson's ventilated head, Packard himself and Mark Edwards all seemed to be mixed up in a gruesome play, while Hazel and Georgina looked on and laughed.

★ ★ ★

It was a little after nine o'clock when he awoke. He lay for a few minutes with the sun shining hotly on his face, then the sound of movement in the flat jerked him properly awake. He had a fleeting memory of his dream, then realization of what it had meant and what had happened in the scrapyard came flooding back to him. The cops! They must have found out that he'd shot Stevenson and they'd come here to —

He fell back on the pillow when he remembered Georgina; the sounds fitted in with the kind of noise she'd make if she were getting breakfast and he grinned because for once he wouldn't have to do it himself.

The sooner he knew more about her, the better he was going to like it.

They didn't talk much over the bacon and eggs and toast which she'd made. He poured himself a second cup of tea.

Georgina looked weary after her night on the settee, but Packard had more important problems than that to worry about, and after gulping down the tea he stood up, doing his best to think like a private detective.

'I'm going to see Hazel,' he said. 'Before I do, I'd better have your address.'

He scribbled it down on a scrap of paper, crumpled it into his pocket then told her not to answer the phone or the door while he was out.

'If I want to call you for any reason,' he said, 'I'll let the phone ring twice, hang up and dial again. That way you'll be certain that it's me.'

She nodded and closed the door as he went out. As soon as she'd fastened it he knelt down on the wooden boards of the corridor and made a careful examination of the lock; at first he could see nothing wrong but finally he managed to make out a few scratches on the metal surround. She'd done a very good job of opening it, one that he would have been proud to have done himself.

His battered old van, which rarely gave

any trouble in spite of its age, was parked in a side street a couple of blocks away, as there had been too many other cars cluttering up the streets nearby for him to get it any closer. Half expecting that Mark Edwards might be hanging about he took great care as he approached it, but there was no one in sight and he was soon on his way to see Hazel.

He parked near her flat and went into the hall, past the postcards which had been pinned on the doorpost by the two old bags upstairs. Hazel's flat was on the second floor; he pressed the illuminated bell push and waited.

The door was opened sooner than he'd expected and as it swung back he grinned, ready to greet Hazel.

'Come in, Packard,' Mark Edwards said, smiling and prodding him with a gun.

6

At about the same time that Lee Packard was driving his battered old van to Hazel Manners' flat, Chief Superintendent Donald Martin was closing the door of his office at Scotland Yard. Inspector Brady was sitting at one of the two desks which had been pushed together in the centre of the room; as the door catch clicked he grinned at Martin, tossed his pencil on to the top of the pile of reports in front of him, and leaned back.

'About time too,' he said. 'There've been more calls so far this morning than I can handle. What kept you?'

Martin hung up his coat and sat down without answering. There wasn't another inspector at the Yard whom he would let speak to him like that; come to think of it, there was probably only Stan Brady who'd try. He was grinning now, and there was little doubt that he'd have made the same remark to almost anyone else who'd come in, from messenger to chief superintendent, and that was one of the reasons why he was still only an inspector, in spite of his record.

'I can't help thinking,' Martin announced, 'that all the calls to this office should be put through while I'm out somewhere.'

'What?' Brady looked up, startled.

'You heard.' The desks formed a big table, and Martin's was the one on the far side, facing the door. He pulled a heap of papers towards him and looked solemnly at Brady.

'Why should we want that?' Brady demanded.

'It's obvious. You could sort out everything then and only give me the important stuff. As it is, I tend to get everything, and I find myself wasting time with all sorts of useless information.'

He kept his face straight as he spoke, and it was a couple of seconds before Brady decided that he was joking.

'I'll take your mind off funny remarks like that,' he said with a sniff. 'Cranbourne was asking for you.'

'When?'

'About fifteen minutes ago. The only thing I could tell him was that you weren't here.'

'I shouldn't worry about it,' Martin said. 'I was here until ten last night and the night before, you know, and they do allow me some time off.' He grinned and began to look through the reports which had come in overnight. 'I'll have a word with him when I've seen what's in here, but if I don't do this first I'll never get chance.'

There wasn't as much in the tray as there had seemed to be, as Brady had taken most of the messages and made a note on each one of what wanted doing, which case it concerned and who was dealing with it. He was one of the most efficient inspectors Martin had ever worked with, and that was one of the reasons why he was allowed to get away with so much; without his help the job would have been a lot harder, and quite a few things might have been overlooked, or at least have taken up valuable time which could be put to better use somewhere else.

'Any idea what Cranbourne wants?' he asked without looking up from the report he was reading.

'Likely to tell me, isn't he?' Brady replied with another sniff. He pulled a handkerchief from his pocket and blew his nose vigorously. 'All I know is that he wants to see you and from the tone of his voice I'd get up there pretty snappy if I were you.'

Martin grinned again.

'Stop worrying, Stan,' he said. 'He doesn't know I'm here yet and you know the mood he's in these days. It'll only be a lot of fuss about something and nothing and if he does phone down again you can take it and tell him that I'm on my way to see him.'

He worked his way steadily through the reports. Normally he wouldn't have been so light-hearted about a call to see the Commander of the C.I.D., but of late Cranbourne seemed to have been obsessed with small things, matters that normally he'd simply have passed out to someone else to deal with; everyone had commented on it, but there was nothing anyone could do.

He was on the last half-dozen reports when the phone rang again. With a quick wink at Brady he thrust the unread forms back into the tray and stood up.

'I'll leave it to you to sweeten him,' he said. 'I'll tell you how successful you were when I get back.'

As he closed the door he heard Brady say:

'Yes, sir. As a matter of fact he's on his way up now, as soon as he got your message.'

Martin hurried along the passage, up the stairs, and tapped on the door before opening it. As he went in, Cranbourne's secretary turned round and frowned at him.

'Good morning, Chief Superintendent,' she said. 'The Commander has been waiting to see you for some time.'

Martin nodded. He wasn't here to argue with secretaries, and if there was any serious complaint Cranbourne would make it himself, especially in his present mood; they could argue it out then.

'I take it he's free now?' he asked.

She nodded, and pressed down a key on the internal telephone as Martin crossed the room and tapped lightly on Cranbourne's door. He opened it without waiting for an answer and stepped inside.

'Good morning, sir.'

'Come in and sit down,' Cranbourne said gruffly. That was no real indication of his mood; anyone could be gruff at this time of the morning without it meaning a thing.

Apologizing would probably be the worst thing that Martin could do, as so far there was nothing which needed an apology, other than some half-baked worry of Brady's. It was a well-known fact about Brady that even though he was so flippant with almost everyone else he actually appeared to fear Commander Cranbourne. Anything that he said had to be done must be started immediately. To delay at all was a crime in Brady's eyes, and to practically ignore the request marked one as a lost man.

'Remember the Wiggin Street bank robbery?' Cranbourne asked abruptly.

Martin nodded.

'I ought to, sir. Four masked men in the bank, a woman customer used as a shield to prevent anyone trying to interfere while they were carrying out the actual robbery, and a passer-by who got in the way was killed. It's one of my cases, of course.'

His voice was bleak as he said that; so far, none of the bandits had been caught, and nothing had been seen of the missing fifty-five thousand pounds.

'I know it's one of your cases,' Cranbourne said testily. 'You don't have to tell me that.'

'It's curious that we haven't turned up any of the money,' Martin mused. 'The organizing was good but from the way that they obviously panicked when they came out of the bank I'd say that they were amateurs, just the type you'd expect to fling the money around.'

Cranbourne watched him, without interrupting.

'I know that we haven't got the numbers of hardly any of the notes, sir,' Martin went on, 'but that kind of person would usually be the type without money originally who'd spend so much of it at once when he got it that we'd be bound to notice. As it is, there's been nothing.'

Now, Cranbourne smiled.

'We have recovered some of the money,' he said.

'Where?' Martin asked sharply.

'A curious case, actually. A man named Stevenson has been murdered in a scrapyard and on the face of it that's all there is to it, but when the Division went round to his room they found some very interesting things.'

Martin waited. Anything could come out of this. What Cranbourne regarded as interesting and what other people regarded as interesting weren't always the same thing.

'Some of the notes whose numbers were known were in a cupboard in Stevenson's bedroom,' Cranbourne said.

'They're definitely the same notes, sir?'

'No doubt about it.' Cranbourne waved his hand. 'That in itself doesn't mean that Stevenson had anything to do with the robbery, of course. He could have been given the notes by someone else, to get rid of them, for instance.'

'That would be risky. He only needs to spend one. With a note that size it would be remembered and the chain leads back from him to the gang.'

'That is the main objection,' Cranbourne said, 'and I don't think that he could be a professional buyer of hot money, either.'

Martin nodded. Most of the people who bought stolen notes had records with the Yard; that was one of the things which made them trustworthy as far as other crooks were concerned, and although Stevenson could be a newcomer it wasn't very likely.

'There is another thing,' Cranbourne went on. 'You remember that apart from the crowbar attack on Walter Deane there were two warning shots fired in the street by another of the gang?'

'That's right, sir. We got two bullets, one from the bank door and one from the window frame of a shop across the road. They haven't been matched with any gun known to us, so far.'

'They've been matched with something now,' Cranbourne said grimly. 'The shot which killed Stevenson was fired from that same gun . . . '

★ ★ ★

Stevenson had lived in the top two rooms of a pokey little house in Whitechapel. Martin arrived there some time after his conversation with Cranbourne, and he and Brady were met by the Divisional man who had been called to the scrapyard, and who had eventually reported the murder to the Yard, Inspector North.

'Good morning,' Martin said.

'Good morning, sir.' North had a clipped, precise voice, as if he were constantly playing the part of an RAF man, and it was obvious from his manner that he was going to be strictly formal. 'Nothing's been disturbed here other than what had to be moved when we were having a look round. Most of it is exactly as Stevenson left it.'

Martin nodded, his eyes going round

the cramped room with its worn carpet, faded wallpaper and furniture which looked as though it might have been new about the time of Queen Victoria. In one corner was a table spread with a dirty cloth, and the wallpaper near it was smeared with butter; one large patch of the wall was even dirtier than the rest, where Stevenson had obviously leaned against it as he was sitting eating. The whole room had a musty, decayed smell about it, and Brady wrinkled up his nose as he came through the door.

'Stinks like a tomb,' he said cheerfully.

Martin smiled. North looked at him, his face completely lacking in expression.

'Nothing has been altered,' he repeated.

In such a room the brand new colour television set looked completely out of place. The polished cabinet gleamed, the controls on the front of it were black and silver and shone so much that there was a faint reflection in them of people moving about the room, and a set of extension controls, allowing the set to be operated from one of the armchairs, had been fitted.

'Wonder where he got that?' Martin asked. If Stevenson had been connected with the bank robbery, then that could be where some of the money had gone.

North permitted himself a grin.

'Wiseman's, the television dealer about half a mile away, was done about two weeks ago. I haven't checked with him yet but I'd say it came from there.'

'Seems likely. Get someone to have a word with him, will you, and let me know. In the meantime, have you spoken with the woman downstairs?'

'Mrs Brooks?' North shook his head. 'She owns the house, sir, and rents these rooms to Stevenson. From what I gather he was some sort of sitting tenant and she couldn't get rid of him. As soon as the notes were found and the report on the gun came through I got straight on to the Yard, and all she knows so far is that Stevenson has been killed.'

'And the body was found in a scrapyard, wasn't it?'

'That's right, sir. I don't know if you've seen the place, which belongs to a character named Spooner. We've had our eye on him for a few months but he's too careful. Doesn't put a foot wrong, or not so's you'd notice.'

'What's he got to say about it?' Martin asked.

'Very cautious, Johnny Spooner,' North said. 'All he can tell us is that when he got to the scrapyard this morning he saw a lot of scuff marks on the ground. It seems that he's been having a lot of trouble with kids getting over the fence at night and playing round all the old cars, and he thought that this was something that they'd been up to. His office is in a wooden hut at the back of the scrapyard, and he saw that there were a couple of furrows leading from the scuff marks to a narrow gap between the hut and the fence. When he followed them to try and find out what had been going on he saw the body.'

North spoke quickly, almost like an official report come to life. When he'd finished he didn't offer any comments but merely waited for Martin to speak.

'I may talk to him later on if it looks as though he can help,' Martin decided, 'but first I'll see what this woman can tell me about Stevenson. What did you say her name was?'

'Mrs Brooks, sir.'

He turned away, heading back to the stairs.

'I'd be glad if you could let me have all the reports as soon as possible,' he said as he went out. 'And can you try and get a list of Stevenson's friends from somewhere? It might come in useful.'

Mrs Brooks wasn't at all the sort of person Martin had been expecting. From what he'd seen of the house he had thought that she'd be middle-aged at least, rough and blowsy, the kind of woman you'd expect to find in an area like this, renting out rooms. Far from it. She was no older than thirty, with an attractive face and a figure that would have stood a very good chance of winning any beauty contest. She wasn't as wary of Martin as most of the people he interviewed were, and she hardly seemed to notice when Brady sat down and opened his notebook.

This room was much better than the one upstairs. The furniture wasn't as old, it had been redecorated fairly recently, and it was swept and dusted regularly. From comparing the two it was easy to say which one had the woman in it, and which was occupied by a man on his own.

'Did you know Mr Stevenson well?' he asked, after he'd introduced himself and Brady, and explained something of what they wanted.

'Not as well as he'd have liked,' she replied. 'A terrible job I had at first, keeping him away, but he soon learned that I wasn't interested.'

'Your husband? Was he friendly with him?'

'He hardly saw him, Mr Martin. That was partly the trouble.'

'In what way?'

'He drives a lorry,' she said, 'and he's away two or three nights a week. Mr Stevenson came with the house or I'd never have dreamed of taking a lodger. As soon as we've got the money we're going to move away from here, into a decent flat in a better area.'

She smiled at him as she said that, and he nodded.

'If you weren't all that friendly with Stevenson I don't suppose you'd know who he went around with, or anything like that? His friends, his girlfriend, even his enemies. Anything could help.'

Dark hair tumbled attractively round her face as she shook her head.

'I don't know many of them, but there was a girl that he knocked around with until the past week or so, and she might be able to tell you more.'

'Got her name?' he asked.

'Of course,' Mrs Brooks replied at once. 'She's called Georgina Lewis.'

7

Outside the door to Hazel's flat, Lee Packard stood with Mark Edwards' mocking words echoing in his ears and his mind searching frantically for a way out and not coming anywhere near finding one.

'Come in, Packard.'

There weren't many answers to an invitation like that, especially when it was made by someone as vicious looking as Edwards and backed up with a gun that he seemed quite ready to use, even in a building like this.

'Come on,' Edwards said impatiently when he didn't move. 'We haven't got all morning.'

'Shoot me,' Packard invited, getting more confidence into his voice than he felt. 'Go on. Pull that trigger and see how many people it brings running.'

Edwards took a quick look along the passage, so fast that there was no chance of taking advantage of the fact that his attention had wandered, and jumping him. When he looked back at Packard the hard expression was still there and there was a sneering twist to his lips.

'People might come running,' he said, 'but I don't think it's very likely. I know the kind of jerks that live here. They won't bother about someone being shot up, as long as it doesn't affect them. They've got problems of their own to worry about.'

Still Packard stayed where he was.

'Move!' Edwards snapped, prodding him again with the gun. 'Or Hazel might get hurt.'

That worked where no threat to himself could have had much effect. He stepped into the hall and Edwards stood to one side so that he could go right in, helping him on his way with a push in the back.

The lounge wasn't at all disarranged. After seeing Edwards at the door Packard had been expecting that there must have been a struggle, but everything seemed to be in its place and the life-sized plastic skull which Hazel kept as a macabre ornament was still grinning at him from its shelf near the phone. The grin looked to have widened this morning, as if it was looking forward to having a companion skull soon.

Packard's.

He took his gaze off it and watched Edwards push the door shut.

'You said last night that you'd broken your leg,' he commented.

'False alarm.' As he went across the room Edwards limped a little but that was the only sign of last night's fall. 'Sit down, Packard.'

By the chair which Hazel normally used was an empty can of beer lying on its side, and a glass which was half-full. Tossed casually on the floor near it was a Batman comic, folded open at an inside page. He sat down in this chair and rustled the pages of the comic with his toe. Batman looked up at him keenly, a confident glint in his eyes, while behind his back a man about eight feet tall and holding a huge knife swung across the street on a long chain hooked to the roof of a skyscraper.

'Where's Hazel?' Packard demanded. 'You said that she was here.'

Edwards shook his head.

'You've got it wrong, pal. All I said was that she might get hurt. Whether she does or not is up to you.'

'How did you know I'd be coming here?'

'It was obvious,' Edwards said, grinning. 'You'd have to see Hazel to find out what she was doing by sending that broad to you. All I did was wait here until you turned up. You came sooner than I thought you would.'

'How long have you been here?' A prickle of alarm at what might have happened to Hazel ran up and down Packard's spine as he asked that.

'An hour or so.' Edwards shrugged. 'That doesn't come into it because with fifty-five thousand quid at stake I'd have waited all day for you.'

As he said that he stared hard at Packard, who managed to keep his face expressionless in spite of the thoughts which were flying through his mind. After watching him for a moment,

Edwards spoke again.

'I'm going to find out where you're hiding Georgina if I have to beat you to a pulp to do it. See that skull up there?' he pointed. 'Yours won't be joining it, because it'll be in too many pieces by the time I've finished.'

'You're going to do that here?' Packard said, trying to grin and not quite succeeding. 'Where's Hazel?'

'She's around, but you won't find her so I should stop worrying.'

'And what about Georgina Lewis? Why do you want her? What's all the fuss about?'

Edwards looked at him, his head on one side. The gun was resting casually on his knee but there was still no chance of jumping him.

'Say that a few more times, Packard, and I'll start to believe you really are in the dark about it all. You mean she hasn't told you?'

'She said she didn't know.'

'So you have got her!' he exclaimed, his eyes narrowing. 'It isn't all a blind.'

'But I don't know anything about it. If

I did I might be able to help you some more.'

Edwards pursed his lips.

'There's no reason why I should tell you any more. All I want to know is where you've put Georgina.'

'Then you'll kill me?'

He nodded.

'So that's a pretty good reason for me not to tell you a thing.'

'You won't be able to help telling me after what I'll do to you,' Edwards said with savage enjoyment. 'And don't forget Hazel, will you?'

'I haven't forgotten her,' Packard said airily, certain now of the way he should play this, 'but isn't there one thing that you've forgotten?'

'I don't think so.'

'All right, let me put it like this. You're going to beat me to a pulp, and while you're doing it you hope that I'll tell you where Georgina is. Suppose I name a place? How do you know that I'm not just shooting off my mouth to stop you hitting me? If you kill me you'll never find her and if you don't, then I can come after you. I've got mates, you know, and they'll back me up.'

Edwards sat back in silence. He seemed to be considering what had just been said, and from the expression on his face he didn't like it. After giving him a few minutes Packard went on:

'Why did you come here to wait for me? Why not go back to my flat?'

'It was easier to come here. You might not have been so willing to open the door if I'd come to your place, but as it was you didn't expect to see me here.'

So they hadn't known that Georgina was at the flat last night, and Edwards still didn't know now. From the way he'd been talking it was obvious that there was big money involved, and what Packard wanted to do now was get his hands on it, or at least find out the full story.

'Look,' he said, 'there's no need for all this talk about beating my head in. I couldn't care less about Georgina. Whatever it is she knows I'll get it out of her whether or not you tell me; the only difference is that you still won't be any the wiser. Even if you kill me, you won't find her, so you're wasting your time.'

Edwards flashed his teeth in a smile.

'You seem to have the whiphand for now,' he said smoothly. 'To put it bluntly she knows where she can put her hands on fifty-five thousand quid.'

Packard's eyes narrowed.

'From the Wiggin Street bank job,' Edwards went on.

Packard frowned, trying to remember; at first the name meant nothing to him, then suddenly he snapped his fingers.

'That's the one that was pulled a month ago, isn't it?' he asked. 'There's a murder rap hung on it.'

Edwards shrugged.

'Maybe there is, but that's nothing to do with me because I didn't pull the job.'

'Then who did?' Packard asked, sarcasm in his voice. 'Don't try and tell me it was Georgina, all on her own.'

'I've no idea. Terry Stevenson had something to do with it but even he didn't know who was behind it.'

'I don't like people who kill innocent passers-by,' Packard declared flatly.

'Neither did Terry. That's why he

argued with them and why they tried to cut him out of his share. Fifty quid he got from that job, Packard, fifty lousy quid, and that in ten pound notes with all the numbers known to the cops.'

'So you're trying to find out where the rest of the money is so you can take the lot?'

Edwards nodded.

'Suppose it's been divided up?'

'It won't have been, not yet. That job was carefully staged and whoever was at the back of it won't let anyone go around flashing sudden wealth, because it points the finger. I know that loot is still intact, and I know that Georgina has a good idea where it is.'

'How?'

'From what Terry Stevenson told me it was obvious that she knew a lot more about the gang than he did. She was on the fringe of it, he thought, and after he split with them we tracked her down and Terry got friendly with her. As soon as she found out what we were really after, she ran.'

Packard laughed.

'So there's a bunch of bank robbers after you, and you're after Georgina. Is that it?'

'Do you think I'd be sitting here talking if I thought that a gang who pulled a job like that knew that I was looking for them? There's no one but Georgina could have told them, anyway, and if she'd been on that friendly terms with them do you think she'd have run from me and Terry? Not on your life. She'd have got them after us, but I haven't seen a sign, so you can bet they don't know.'

'And what exactly do you want from me?'

Edwards didn't move. His eyes blinked slowly and the gun remained pointing at Packard.

'I want you to tell me where Georgina is, and then I want to find out from her where the money's hidden.'

'Suppose she doesn't know?'

'She knows,' he said viciously. 'She's trying to play it cool but she isn't experienced enough to work in this league.'

'What makes you think you are?'

Packard laughed softly then dropped his hand to the glass of beer which was by the chair, snatched it up and flung it at Edwards.

Edwards was a fraction late in moving. The glass caught him in the face and as he tried to get out of the way he went over backwards in the chair. There was a crash as he hit the carpet and the beer glass shattered, spraying the remaining contents over the floor. At the same moment Packard jumped forward, intent on grabbing the gun.

Edwards's arms came round him like steel bands and he felt the cold touch of the gun as it was pressed against his neck. The picture of himself and Terry Stevenson fighting last night came vividly into his mind. His eyes bulged, then he heaved and the chill touch vanished. He smashed his fist into Edwards's face. Edwards grunted and the gun bounced across the floor. Instinctively Packard turned to see where it was going and Edwards heaved, throwing him off. Packard rolled over and carried on rolling, reaching the gun which had gone under the table, before Edwards could get up. He grabbed it as Edwards got to his knees.

'That's right,' Packard said, gasping for breath. 'You'd better stay like that and pray that I don't shoot you.'

Edwards rubbed the back of his hand over his face where he had been hit, and tried to get up.

'I said stay there,' Packard told him sharply. 'Move again and you'll get a bullet in your leg. That won't be a false alarm.'

'You wouldn't shoot,' Edwards sneered, but he didn't have enough faith in his judgement to take a chance. He sank back on to his knees, staring up.

'Where's Hazel?' Packard demanded.

'You'll never find her,' he said, then came up off the floor like an uncoiling spring, using his feet for extra speed. The whole thing was done so fast that Packard had no time to get out of the way and couldn't have pulled the trigger even if he'd wanted to. Edwards hit him with his shoulder, sending him against the wall, cracking his nose against it and making him drop the gun.

Edwards didn't wait to pick it up. As Packard struggled to keep conscious he heard the door being opened and then a sound of running footsteps along the passage.

He forced himself to move, not even pausing to pick up the gun himself. Edwards knew where Hazel was and that was the one thing which could hold up Packard's plans now. He had to find out where she was and get her back before he could do anything else. Wrenching open the door which Edwards had slammed after him, he was just in time to see him opening another door at the end of the passage.

As he went through it he looked round, a faint smile on his face, then he banged the door after him. By the time Packard had struggled towards it and opened it, his head throbbing more and more with each movement, Edwards was nowhere in sight.

Packard leaned against the wall. Where he had the advantage over Edwards was that he had been here a lot and knew the layout of the building. Just ahead of him was a large landing, with stairs leading up and down. There was a back entrance which could be reached from here by going down the steps, while going up led only to the roof, with no way back again except by these same stairs.

So if Edwards had gone down he would probably get away; if he had gone up towards the roof he was trapped and could be picked up at leisure.

Packard went forward until he came on to the landing itself. Sunshine streamed in through the window which looked on to the car park and at the other side was a big cupboard which was used by the caretaker.

It was as he passed this that he heard a faint sound.

He stopped at once, listening. The noise came again, very faintly. It could have been caused by anything, and it made the hairs on the back of his neck crawl. If Mark Edwards had slipped in there he had made a mistake, and Packard began to grin.

Walking on his toes so that he wouldn't

make any sound he moved towards the cupboard. He didn't know whether or not Edwards could see out, but that was a chance he'd have to take. The sound appeared to have stopped now but he moved on until he was standing right in front of the door, then put his ear against it carefully and listened.

There was silence.

He began to think he had imagined the earlier sounds. Stepping to one side so that the door would hide him as it opened he reached up and turned the knob. The cupboard wasn't locked and there was no resistance. As it swung open the crack between the hinges and the post widened, until he could look through it without being seen.

Mark Edwards wasn't inside the cupboard.

Instead, Packard saw a girl, her hands tied and a piece of sticking plaster over her mouth.

8

It was Hazel Manners. He didn't realize that at first, but after moving to a position where he could see her face it was obvious. He stared at her for a moment then stepped round the cupboard door and stared down at her. She was lying on the bottom of the cupboard, on her back, her knees drawn up so that she would fit into the space and her hands tied in front of her. The sticking plaster over her mouth had been stuck down firmly and was so wide that it almost covered her nose too. Her eyes were open and she was looking up with a fixed terror. For a moment he thought that she might be dead but then he saw that she was breathing.

'It's only me, Hazel,' he said, too stunned to think of anything better.

A hint of recognition appeared in her eyes and the terror faded slightly. Suddenly her lips began to move beneath the broad band of plaster and though he couldn't make out the words he could guess their sense easily enough from the expression on her face.

Stooping, he pulled at the sticking plaster. After a few attempts he got his fingernail under a corner of it, lifted it slightly and tore it off. Hazel gasped, then worked her mouth. Little pieces of adhesive backing were left around her lips, giving her an odd, blotched appearance.

'Get these damned ropes off,' she said as soon as she could speak.

He nodded and took out his knife. It wasn't very sharp but after sawing at the cords for a few seconds he began to cut through them strand by strand. Hazel watched impatiently, then shook them off stiffly. She flopped about on the floor of the cupboard then grunted.

'You'll have to help me up,' she said. 'I can't move.' There was an edge of terror in her voice, and panic in her eyes.

'You'll be all right in a minute when the cramp's worn off,' he told her. 'Give me your arm.'

She gave another gasp of pain as he pulled her to her feet, then clung to him as she stepped out of the cupboard.

'Where's Edwards?' she demanded thickly, still clutching his arm.

'He's gone. He was in your flat, waiting for me to turn up, but I bounced him. I've no idea where he's gone now, and I didn't know where you were until I heard something moving in the cupboard. I thought you were him, hiding.'

'I've been in there for hours,' she said as they moved very slowly along the passage, Hazel staggering, Packard doing his best to hold her upright. 'I've been trying to make a noise but I got so stiff that I could hardly move.'

Packard didn't reply. It was taking all his attention to stop her from falling. When they were nearly at her door he saw one of the girls who lived upstairs coming towards them. Hazel managed a ghastly smile and the girl winked at Packard.

'Drunk, so early in the morning, dear?' she said in a thin whining voice which didn't go at all well with her well-padded appearance. 'I don't know how you manage it.'

She walked on and Hazel muttered something. The door of her flat was still open and as they went in Packard kicked it shut. It slammed and he helped Hazel into the living-room. She looked dully at the shattered beer glass, wrinkled her nose at the smell caused by the spilled beer, and flopped into a chair.

Going over to the cabinet Packard mixed a couple of strong drinks. He handed one to her and she swallowed most of it at a gulp.

'That's better,' she said, wiping away with her hand some that was trickling down her chin. 'I'd like to see her if she'd spent most of the night in a cupboard.'

'You've been in there most of the night?' Packard demanded in a hard voice.

She nodded, finished off the drink and reached for the bottle to pour another one.

'I was just setting off to go to that modelling job when the bell rang. It was Georgina Lewis.' Her voice sharpened, and he could see she was recovering quickly. 'You've seen her, haven't you?'

He nodded.

'She's safe, don't worry. She's worth fifty-five thousand quid to us, Hazel.'

'You haven't been idle, have you?' she said, speaking more clearly and looking much better now that the whisky was having an effect.

'I'll tell you about that in a minute,' he said impatiently. 'What happened to you?'

'Georgina came. I hadn't seen her for well over a year, perhaps even longer, but that didn't worry her. She wanted to know if she could stay with me for a few days, because two men were chasing her. I hadn't much time because I was rushing off to a modelling job but I was interested, and when I found out that one of the men was Mark Edwards I was even more interested.'

'Do you know him?' Packard asked sharply.

'I've heard of him. He used to run with Flanaghan's mob, and I reckoned that if it was worth his while to chase her there must be money in it somewhere.'

Packard nodded. He'd heard of Flanaghan, one of the big-time mobsters. At one time he'd tried to work for him, but Flanaghan hadn't been interested in a small-time dip.

'He's not with Flanaghan now, is he?' he asked.

Hazel shook her head.

'I said that she could stay here if she wanted,' she went on, 'but that we'd better make sure she hadn't been followed. When we looked out of the window we saw Edwards across the road. It wasn't safe for her to stay here then, and I suggested that she could go to you. I told her you were a private detective and that you'd help her without running to the cops, whatever trouble she was in.'

'Why didn't you phone me and try and give me a bit of warning?'

'There wasn't time,' she said simply. 'I was already late and there was still the matter of getting Georgina out of the house without Edwards seeing her. In the end we arranged that she'd go out the back way while I held him at the front, asking him the way or something. We thought that he wouldn't know me but he was smarter than that. He knew me all right and I'd only asked him if he knew where Foster Street was when a car pulled alongside us. They pushed me in it, Edwards and one of his mates, a man called Terry, and drove me around for a while.'

She pushed up her hair and showed him a large bruise and scratch on her neck.

'In the end,' she went on, 'I had to tell them that I'd sent her to you.'

'The swines!' Packard said. He gazed blankly at the opposite wall for a minute and then looked back to her. 'What did they do then?'

'They brought me back here and put me in that cupboard. The next thing I knew was that you were looking down at me.'

'The swines,' he repeated.

'Any chance of some food?' Hazel demanded. 'And I've missed that modelling job now. It could have led to big things if I'd done it properly.'

'You may have missed the modelling

job, honey, but you won't need things like that when we've got fifty-five thousand quid under our belts.'

'What are you talking about? What's been happening while I've been in that cupboard?'

She sat in the chair while he cooked eggs and bacon and made a big pot of tea and told her everything that had taken place. She didn't interrupt at all and he could see that she was working out how each move could fit into her own plans as he told her about it. When he had finished she leaned back. In the kitchen the kettle shrilled.

'So Georgy girl can lead us to fifty-five thousand quid,' she said. 'Are you sure she's safe, Lee? I'd hate Mark Edwards to find her while we're sitting here, talking.'

'She's safe,' he assured her as he put the finishing touches to the meal. 'My flat's the last place they'll think of looking. They'll be expecting me to do something clever.'

Hazel laughed, a short barking sound.

'If they're waiting for that, they'll wait a

long time. They don't know you as well as I do.'

'There's no need for that. Let's concentrate on getting our hooks on this cash.'

'Fifty-five thousand quid,' Hazel said softly. 'We could do a lot with that. I could get out of this dump for a start.'

'You could buy it if you wanted,' he agreed. 'Don't forget we've to get the stuff first.'

Hazel's eyes narrowed. She ate quickly, not making any answer to that while Packard sat and watched her, thoughts about the money going round his head. When she had finished the meal Hazel leaned back and sighed.

'That's better,' she said. 'I can think more easily now.' The marks of the plaster were still round her mouth, though the grooves that the cords had made on her wrists had faded. After sitting for a moment she went into the bathroom and began to sponge her lips carefully.

'Where do we go from here?' Packard said, sitting on the edge of the bath. 'And what about Edwards? I'd like to smash his face to a pulp after what he did to you.'

'We'll deal with him when he crops up again,' she said shortly. 'I wonder why he hasn't come back?'

Packard shrugged.

'Perhaps he's had enough for now. He'll be back, don't worry. What I'm more concerned about are the people who ran this bank job in the first place. Think they'll interfere?'

'I shouldn't think so,' she said, drying her mouth. 'If they'd been going to they'd have been after Edwards in the first place.'

They went back into the living-room. Packard looked round quickly then saw the gun beneath the table. He picked it up and rested it in the palm of his hand.

'Could come in useful,' he said.

'Is that the one that killed Stevenson?'

'How do I know? Does it matter?'

'Get rid of it,' Hazel said. 'It could be a clincher if the cops find us.'

'How are they going to come into it?' Packard demanded. 'Talk sense, Hazel.' He dropped the gun into his pocket and sat down. In the comic at his feet Batman was still looking confident and it was obvious that he had no idea that the big guy was swinging down the chain. The next picture was on the following page but Packard was willing to bet that the smile would be wiped off his face when he found out what was going on behind him.

'There's no time to read comics,' Hazel said, seeing him looking down at it. 'What you've got to do now is go back home and talk to Georgina. What you'll have to do is make her think you can help her, but for God's sake don't let her imagine that you've any intentions of taking the money off her.'

'She thinks I'm a private detective, thanks to you,' Packard grinned. 'That gives me the excuse to ask any questions that I think of. She's even going to pay me for asking them!'

'We'll send her a bill,' Hazel said absently. 'You'd better keep in touch with me in case Edwards comes back here.'

Packard caught his breath. It hissed and rattled in his throat. That was something he hadn't thought of in the excitement of being so close to so much money.

'Hadn't you better come and stay with me?' he asked. 'That should be safer and at least I'll know what's going on if anything does happen.'

'And how much room have you got at your place?' she said with a sneer. 'You're going to have your hands full with Georgina there. You'd better keep your hands off her, too.'

He grinned.

'She's a well stacked piece.'

'I'm the only piece you need,' Hazel said softly. 'Don't get any fancy ideas, Lee.'

'Quit worrying.'

'I'm just making sure,' she said. 'Don't worry about Edwards. I was taken by surprise before and that won't happen again. You concentrate on making sure he doesn't get Georgy girl and I'll look after myself.'

Not long afterwards, Packard left. He was still carrying the gun in his pocket, though Hazel had insisted that he get rid of it as soon as he could, just in case there was any connection between it and last night's shooting. That had almost gone from his mind now. It was as if it had happened to someone else and he was fairly confident that it would never be connected with him.

There was no sign of Edwards, which was reassuring. He started the car and drove home. No one followed him, and he made a detour on the way so that he could drop the gun into the river.

This time, he managed to drive right up to the house instead of having to park his car a few streets away. Hurrying up the stairs, he wondered what he would say to Georgina. He would have to be careful not to let it slip how much he knew about the money, and to act as if he only had the information she'd given him.

He opened the door and went in casually, then stopped. It didn't need much in the way of observation to know that the flat was empty and Georgina had gone.

9

There was no need for a search; the flat wasn't that big, and anyway it had that hollow, empty sort of noise which he was so used to and which told him at once that he was alone. Still, it was better to make sure before he started off a lot of panic, and he went first into the bedroom, then the bathroom.

There was no one.

He ran his hand over his face. His late night last night, the fight in the scrapyard and the trouble afterwards with Georgina and then Edwards this morning, were taking their toll now and he felt bewildered. His first impulse was to call Hazel and see what she had to say, then he decided to wait a few minutes and to try and work things out for himself.

There would have been time for Mark Edwards to have come here after leaving Hazel's flat, and kidnap Georgina, but to do that he would have had to know where she was, and then get into the flat. Packard had told her not to answer the door or the phone but women were stupid at the best of times and she needn't have taken any notice of what he'd said. Edwards could have her and that would explain why they hadn't seen him again back at Hazel's, but —

He looked round the room once more.

That was when he spotted the note.

It didn't look much, just a small white square propped above the fireplace, almost hidden by the jumble of other stuff that was on there. Standing up, he went over to it. It was simply a sheet of his own notepaper, folded over once and leaned against the wall.

He opened it.

'I've gone back to my own flat for a few clothes if you want me for anything,' it said, in small, girlish handwriting. Her address followed, and then the signature, clearly readable. Georgina Lewis.

For a few seconds he actually forgot about the fifty-five thousand pounds they were hoping she would lead them to. All he could think about was that while he was dashing all over the place, being beaten up by Mark Edwards and getting drawn into murder, she was calmly going back to her flat as if nothing had happened. He stood with his hands clenched at his side, read the note again, then crumpled it into his pocket and went over to the phone.

Hazel answered very quickly and in a breathless voice, as if she had run to grab the receiver.

'Seen anything of Edwards?' he asked her.

'Not a thing.' Her voice sharpened. 'Why do you ask that? Is something wrong?'

'I've a note from Georgina,' he told her. 'She says that she's gone to her flat. Do you think I should get over there and see what's going on, or leave her to it and wait here till she comes back?'

There was a pause at the other end of the line. Above the hum of the telephone he could hear Hazel breathing, gasping almost, and when she finally spoke there was a definite note of panic in her voice.

'How long ago did she leave?'

'I've no idea,' he said. 'I've just got in, and she'd left a note.'

'I should get over there,' she said with sudden decision. 'There's no telling what she might be planning and we don't want to let that girl out of our sight. She's worth fifty-five thousand quid to us, and don't you forget it.'

'I'm not likely to.'

'The thing that worries me,' Hazel said slowly, 'is that Mark Edwards might have thought it would be worth keeping a watch on her place. If he did, then she'll have walked right into him.'

'And we've lost her,' Packard said grimly. 'I'll go over right now and call you when I've got something.'

He dropped the receiver back on to its cradle and stood for a few seconds with his hand on it. Then, deciding that there was no point in wasting time, he took out the note again, checked the address and thrust it back into his pocket.

Of course, he already had her address which she'd given him before he'd gone to see Hazel, but it was encouraging that she'd repeated it on the note. If nothing else, it didn't suggest that she'd walked out of here with the intention of disappearing.

He ran down the stairs and out to his car. She didn't live too far away and even with the mid-morning traffic to slow him down he didn't reckon it would take above twenty minutes to get there.

In fact, it took him nearer half an hour.

On the way, thoughts about Georgina churned through his mind. The silly bitch was up to something, he was sure. She was trying to take them for a ride, there was more to it than there appeared to be on the surface; Packard could see the money slipping through his slim, deft, and heavily insured fingers if he didn't do something.

At last he turned into the street where Georgina lived. It didn't look to be a much better district than the one in which his own flat was situated, and the house was very similar. He couldn't park in the drive because of a couple of other cars which were there and he lost another few minutes driving round the mean streets.

Crummy little houses like this, he thought, yet a car at every door and nowhere to park. Eventually he found a spot, locked up the car and hurried back.

It was slightly chilly in the entrance hall, as if it was never heated. A board on the wall listed the tenants, but he had no need of that. He went straight up the stairs, his legs working like pistons, and reached the first floor landing, and the short passage which ran off it.

By now, he had convinced himself that there was some plot afoot to cheat him. He hurried along the passage. Georgina's door was almost at the end, and he rapped on it impatiently. When there was no answer he thumped on it with his clenched fist, then realized that he was working himself up into a temper and was going to be at a disadvantage when he met her again.

He dropped his hands to his sides and waited.

There was a sound of footsteps and the door opened.

Packard started to speak, but then the words died on his lips. The smile which he had fixed on his face vanished. He felt as he had done as a child, one time, when a cricket ball had hit him in the stomach.

'Yes, sir?' the policeman who had opened the door asked politely.

Packard swallowed. The copper didn't seem to have noticed that there was anything odd in his manner, but you could never be sure. He had that standard cop face, and behind it he could have been thinking anything.

'I'd like to see Georgina Lewis, if she's in,' he said firmly, struggling to control his emotions.

'What name is it, sir?'

'Packard,' he said after a moment. 'Lee Packard.'

'Are you a friend of hers?'

He nodded.

The expression on the policeman's face didn't change. Opening the door wider he told Packard to come into the flat; feeling that if he did so he might not get out again it was on the tip of his tongue to refuse, then he realized that would only make things worse, and that if the cop wasn't suspicious now, he would be then.

He stepped into the hall and the door slammed behind him.

'I'm afraid there's been a bit of trouble, Mr Packard, but the superintendent will tell you everything you want to know.'

Packard stood in what was obviously the living-room, his heart thudding, his breathing shallow. It was a better flat than his own, but not much. The furnishings had that dingy sameness about them, and the walls could have done with some new paper or a lick of paint. After he had been standing there for a few minutes a door at the other side of the room opened and a tall, well-built man wearing a dark brown suit came out.

His every movement showed that he was a cop; he had that way of looking at people that only came after long years in uniform, though when he looked at Packard there was nothing hard in it.

'I'm Chief Superintendent Martin,' he said. 'You wanted to see Miss Lewis, did you?'

Controlling his urge to run, but not trusting his voice, Packard nodded.

'I'm afraid she's dead, sir,' Martin said. 'She was murdered some time this morning.'

10

Martin stared curiously at the man in front of him, trying to figure out what was wrong; somehow he looked agitated, and his reaction to the news that Georgina had been killed wasn't quite right. There was nothing he could put his finger on, but the uniformed man had come back into the room and was staring too, as if he thought the same thing.

Perhaps there was nothing and it was just imagination, for after all there was no telling how close to the dead girl Packard had been, and this could have come as something of a shock to him.

'Murdered?' Packard demanded.

'I'm sorry, Mr Packard,' Martin said gently. 'She was stabbed, and there's no doubt that she'd have been killed instantly.' He paused, giving Packard time to digest that and then asked: 'Did you know her well?'

Packard looked as if he were struggling

to pull himself together. When he spoke again his voice was much stronger than it had been, not as stupid sounding, and with more of his normal character in it.

'Not all that well,' he said. 'We were friends, but that's about all.'

'How about her other friends? Know many of them?'

Packard shook his head, then said:

'How did you come to find her? What happened?'

'We wanted to see her in connection with some other enquiries we're making,' Martin said smoothly. 'I called round, and when I got here there was no answer to my knock so I went to the flat next door. The neighbour said that Georgina was away but she remembered hearing a lot of noise coming from the flat not long before I called. She didn't think anything of it but I decided to take a look.' He paused. 'I had to break the door open, and when I'd done so I found Georgina in the bedroom, dead.'

'I see.'

There was another pause.

Martin still stared at Packard, remembering how the neighbour had yapped away, anxious to make excuses for the fact that she hadn't been going to do anything about the noises from the supposedly empty flat. Martin had sensed as soon as she had mentioned them that something was wrong; even on its own it would have warranted investigation, but combined with the tie-in to the Wiggin Street robbery it was certain that there was something badly amiss.

By now, the body had been taken away and the team of experts had almost finished their work in the bedroom. There was a chalk outline marking the position of the body, endless photographs of it and the bloodstains and the surroundings, and a light sprinkling of grey fingerprint powder was everywhere in the flat.

As far as Martin knew nothing had been missed; the fingerprint check would probably prove useless because even the dimmest crook took care over things like that these days, but it still had to be done. Harder than finding the killer's prints, if there were any, would be the elimination of the dozens of others they would find, a tedious, routine job, but not one that he would have to do.

That was one blessing.

Packard hadn't moved.

'Can I ask you why you wanted to see her, Mr Packard?'

'No particular reason,' Packard answered with a shrug. 'I was just passing and I thought I might as well slip in. To tell you the truth I thought I might get a cup of tea out of it.'

Martin nodded.

'Didn't you know that she was away, then, and had been since early last week?'

'No. I haven't seen her for almost a month, and she hadn't made any arrangements then.'

He lied fluently and well; there was nothing in the way he said that to make Martin think it was anything but the truth. The silly bitch must have told the neighbours she was going away when she'd gone on the run from Edwards and Stevenson. It was as good a thing as any to say, and it would keep the wagging tongues quiet for a while.

'How long have you known her?' Martin asked.

'Not long, say about six months.'

'And you've no idea who her other friends are?'

'I've already told you, no. I'd like to help you, but I can't tell you things I don't know, can I?'

He put a simpering smile on his face. It was one he had practised often and which he used on the rare occasion when his victims felt a tug at their pockets and turned round to see what was going on. It made him look slightly simple, and immediately explained everything to their way of thinking; he used it now and saw Martin's face clear.

'Where do you live, Mr Packard?'

Packard gave his address; however simple he might make himself out to be, there was no way in which he could avoid that. After writing it down, Martin said:

'I don't think we'll be needing you for anything else sir, but if we do I'll get in touch with you.'

He watched Packard walk, hurry almost, to the door and go out, then turned and went back into the bedroom. Identification of the body had been easy, as the neighbour who had told them about the noises had been only too happy to come in, so that she could see what was going on.

As Martin went into the room now and closed the door Brady, who was standing by a bedside cabinet, looked up, a small, blue covered book in his hand.

'Well?' he asked.

'I don't think he'll be much help to us. If you ask me he's a bit simple. Didn't seem to understand half of what I was saying, and the half that did get through to him he couldn't answer.'

Brady flipped over the pages of the book he was holding.

'This seems to be some sort of address book. What was that character's name?'

'Lee Packard.'

'He isn't listed in here,' Brady said after a moment. 'Think that means anything?'

Martin shrugged.

'It means that either she didn't keep her address book up to date or he isn't as friendly with her as he seemed to think he was. What probably happened was that he tried to pick her up in a dance hall once and she gave him her address to shut him up.'

'Could be,' Brady said, pursing his lips. 'Can't see her giving him her address though if she didn't fancy him, can you?'

'Perhaps not. Is there anything else in that book that might be useful?'

He left the point of Packard's address; they wouldn't get anywhere by arguing about it now, and if it turned out to be important it could always be checked later.

'Not much, as far as I can see. She didn't seem to have many friends and it shouldn't take the Divisions long to go round and have a word with them. Stevenson's is listed, so that seems to fit with her being his girlfriend, and there's one other you might like to see for yourself.'

'Who's that?'

'The bloke she worked for, name of Cummins. You never know, he might be able to tell us something useful.'

'We'll try him afterwards,' Martin decided. 'Another thing we want to check is whether any of Stevenson's friends are in that book, and then see if any of them have a record. We could get something that way.'

With the departure of the rest of the team, the fingerprint men, the doctor, the photographers and the like, the flat seemed very quiet. While Martin took charge of the main line of the investigation and tried to see how it fitted in with the Wiggin Street robbery, they would sift everything they had found and eventually their reports would arrive on his desk.

He sighed. Sometimes it seemed to him that his life was made up of one report after another, with no way of ever slowing down the amount.

'You don't sound too hopeful of finding anything,' Brady commented.

'I'm not.' He grinned suddenly, though he didn't feel very amused. 'I wonder what Georgina did for Cummins?'

'I've no idea,' Brady said, 'but surely she could have found something better? If

I had to live in surroundings like this, I'd feel like giving up. He must have paid her a decent wage, surely?'

'She might not have wanted to spend it on where she lived,' Martin said. 'We aren't all as houseproud as you are.' He glanced at his watch. 'Let's get back to the Yard now, and then after lunch we'll go and see Cummins and find out if he knows anything. I'd like to know where she was spending this week away that she's just had, for one thing.'

'And why she came back without any luggage,' Brady said as they went down the stairs and out to the car. 'There wasn't a suitcase in the flat. Funny, isn't it, if she's just been away?'

The police car was parked in the drive, and was one of those which had stopped Packard from getting in; had he not been in such a hurry and had stopped to look more closely he would probably have recognized it for what it was, even though it was a plain car.

They didn't talk much on the journey back to the Yard. Brady was concentrating on driving, while Martin turned over all

116

the facts he had so far, trying to make them fit and make sense; there seemed to be a vague pattern, but he couldn't see it clearly, and he knew that he would have to turn up a lot more before the end to this case was in sight.

They reached the Yard and went up the stairs to his office; while they had both been out a sergeant had been left in charge, and as the door opened he turned to see who was coming in. When he saw Martin he stood up.

'I've left all the messages on the pad, sir,' he said. 'I don't think there's anything urgent. And this envelope has come in from Inspector North.'

Martin sat down as the sergeant went out, leaving the envelope on one side while he looked through the other things, tossing most of them into the basket for Brady to look at later, and marking one or two with action that he wanted taking. Eventually he reached the envelope from North at the Division and tore it open.

'This is the list of Terry Stevenson's friends that I asked him to get for me,' he said to Brady as he unfolded it. 'Can you have a look at it while I get something to eat and see if any of the names match with Georgina's address book?'

Pinned to the list was a note.

'Television from Wiseman's, as we thought,' it said.

Martin stared at it, puzzled, then remembered the new colour set which had been in Stevenson's rooms, and the break-in at the dealer's; at least that hadn't been bought with money stolen from the bank.

If Stevenson had had a share of the bank money, would he have bothered about a job like that? Maybe, if he hadn't wanted to flash his other money round, but needed something to live on. And if he hadn't been connected with Wiggin Street, how come he'd been shot with the same gun?

He went up to the dining-room, leaving Brady with the list. As soon as he got back, he knew from the gleam in Brady's eye that he'd found something, and stood by the door, waiting.

'Only one name's common,' Brady

said, 'and he's got a record.' He flicked an official photograph across the desk. 'There he is. His name's Mark Edwards, if that means anything to you. It doesn't to me.'

11

There was nothing wrong with Steven Cummins that a few square meals wouldn't put right. That was the first thought that came into Martin's mind when he saw him, a tall, very thin man with haggard, sunken cheeks as though some secret worry had been preying on his mind for most of his life. His black hair was thick and glossy, giving an odd effect perched on top of that body, and his bright eyes darted from side to side, as if they were determined not to miss anything that might be going on.

The office was better than Martin had expected. He had had a lot of experience of one-man firms in the district where Cummins was, and he had been visualizing a shabby, run-down place, especially when he had seen that Cummins was described in the phone book as an 'agent'. There was nothing else to show what kind of business he carried on, and that was one of the points Martin wanted to clear up.

There was no shabbiness. Instead there was a comfortable, well-appointed room at the top of a narrow flight of stairs. The carpet on the floor was reasonably thick, with a bright pattern on it that wasn't too worn, and the desk, while not new, was large and shiny.

There was everything you'd expect to find in an office, and hanging on the wall was a calendar with a picture on it of a girl wearing just a pair of red gloves and the bottom half of a red bikini. She was something else that didn't fit in with the sight of Cummins, who looked as though women would mean no more to him than the spent match which he had just carefully broken into four pieces while talking to Martin.

'You say that Georgina has been murdered?' he asked, lining up the bits of the match along the edge of the blotter on his desk.

'I'm afraid so.'

'That's a little drastic, isn't it?'

Cummins asked. 'Are you sure that it wasn't an accident?'

'She was stabbed,' Martin replied. 'It doesn't give the impression of having been done accidentally.'

Cummins sat back, his face pale. He shivered for a second or two and then seemed to recover.

'I won't pretend that she was a close friend of mine,' he said. 'Actually she was just an employee, kept very much to herself.'

'Had she worked here long?'

'Almost a year.' Cummins paused. 'But why have you come to me? How can I help you?'

'I'm after any information about her that I can get,' Martin said. 'All we seem to have found out so far is that she worked for you and she was away last week.'

'That's right. She had the week off. She should have started work again the day after tomorrow.'

'Did she say where she was going, or what she intended doing?'

Cummins shook his head.

'From what I gathered she wasn't going anywhere, but simply having the time off. She told me she had a lot of jobs to clear up at home and she was hoping to get some of those done.' He gave a faint smile. 'She was only young, Mr Martin, and you know what girls of that age are like. If a boyfriend had come along with something that sounded more attractive than doing jobs about the house she'd have gone with him.'

'I know what you mean,' Martin said. Georgina hadn't looked much older than his own daughter, Beverley, and he knew that she could never be relied upon to stick to a plan from one week to the next. The fact that Georgina had told Cummins she was staying at home and the neighbours that she was going away didn't mean a thing. She could have gone anywhere, or done anything.

'Did you know her boyfriend?' he asked carefully.

'Which one?'

'How many were there?' It was his turn to be taken by surprise.

'Quite a few, from what she used to say.

I think the most recent was Terry Stevenson.'

'Was Mark Edwards one of them?' Martin asked quickly.

'I never heard the name, but that's nothing to go on.'

Martin hesitated, thinking back over his trip to Edwards' flat. There had been no answer to his ring at the bell, and although in the circumstances that was suspicious there were no grounds for getting a search warrant or anything like that; all he had been able to do was leave a constable on watch, with a copy of the photograph and instructions not to show himself, and see what happened.

Mark Edwards was one problem.

Whether or not to tell Cummins that Stevenson was dead was another.

He decided not to, at least not yet, so that he could get to know what Cummins had thought about him without his answers being coloured in any way.

'Did you see Stevenson?' he asked.

'He came here once or twice to collect Georgina after work, but that was all I saw of him.'

'What impression did you get?'

Cummins looked towards the window. At this time of day the sun shone right into it, and a cream coloured linen blind was pulled half-way down. The pieces of the broken match were still on the blotter, and he pushed two of them out of line with his fingernail, until they fell on to the surface of the desk itself. With a sudden movement he swept them all up and dropped them into the waste-paper basket, where they made a tiny clatter as they fell.

'I saw so little of him that it was difficult to form an impression,' he said. 'In any case, I find it difficult to form impressions of people just like that. It never seems to worry me when I'm doing business with a man, but outside that I always have trouble.'

'Exactly what business are you in, Mr Cummins?'

Cummins smiled.

'I'm an agent.'

'For what?'

'I act as agent between people who have something to sell or something to offer, and those who wish to buy.'

'Surely there isn't much call for that sort of thing?'

'You'd be surprised,' Cummins said. 'A builder knows where to buy bricks, an engineering firm knows where it can sell the things it makes, but the things I deal in are more unusual than that.'

'In what way?'

'In any way,' Cummins replied vaguely. 'I've just got rid of a big consignment of tropical fish, for instance. None of the zoos wanted them, the pet shops couldn't take enough to dispose of them all, but I found buyers. Another thing I did was find an old, horse-drawn bus for someone who was running a carnival. They aren't spectacular deals, Mr Martin, but you'd be surprised how many people are willing to pay good money to someone who can do deals like that.'

It sounded a vague, hit and miss kind of business to Martin, but he supposed that there must be a demand or Cummins would never have been able to survive.

'Let me put it this way, Mr Cummins.

Would you have done business with Stevenson?'

Cummins brushed back a lock of his thick, wavy hair. He looked sadly at the blotter, then slowly shook his head.

'I don't think I would, Mr Martin,' he said. 'There's nothing I can put my finger on but there was something about him which made me think he might be a bad risk.' He paused. 'My business isn't the kind that can afford bad risks and I have to be careful who I deal with.'

'I see,' Martin said, pursing his lips. He had the feeling that Cummins hadn't liked to say that about Stevenson and that he would have preferred to say he would willingly deal with him, and had found nothing wrong with the young man. He was about to ask another question when Cummins said:

'I don't think he'd kill Georgina, if that's what you're thinking. You say that she was stabbed?'

'That's right.'

'I can't help you there, either. I never saw him with a knife but it's hardly the thing he'd produce in here, is it?' He gave a short, dry laugh.

'Maybe not. Tell me, Mr Cummins, do you know a friend of Georgina's named Lee Packard?'

'Packard?' Cummins frowned. 'I don't think so, but getting back to Stevenson, haven't you seen him yourself? Why ask my opinion of him?'

'He's dead too, I'm afraid,' Martin said.

Cummins jerked back as if he'd been slapped across the face with one of his own tropical fish that he was trying to sell. He started to say something, closed his mouth for a moment and then tried again.

'This is monstrous, Mr Martin. The police — '

'We're doing everything we can.'

Cummins stared at him then raised his eyebrows slowly; it was as if they were very heavy and his thin body could hardly find the strength to move them.

There was a deep silence in the room, and the sudden, jarring ring of the phone bell sounded exceptionally loud Cummins reached out and picked up the receiver, almost whispering into it, so that his words didn't carry into the room. This was an unconscious habit, for he was so used to discussing his curious deals with people over the phone while possible rivals were sitting on the other side of the desk that he automatically dropped his voice whenever he spoke on the phone; suddenly he laid the receiver on the desk, holding it with his hands clamped over both ends, so that none of the conversation in this office would be heard through it.

'This call is for you,' he said. 'An Inspector Brady, calling from your office.'

Frowning, Martin took the receiver from him, wondering what was so urgent that he had to be interrupted here.

'Hello, Stan,' he said briskly. 'What can I do for you?'

'Sorry to drag you away from the whispering wonder,' Brady said, 'but Edwards has turned up and there's a bit of trouble over at his place. I think you ought to get over there right away.'

12

P.C. Raymond Atkinson was bored. He crouched miserably in front of the house where Edwards had his flat; following his instructions he was hidden in the bushes, thinking of his girlfriend and of what he could be doing if he was with her instead of being stuck outside this dump, and mentally composing a letter of resignation which he knew would never be sent.

He had been on the force for twelve months, and had spent much of that time trying to get a transfer to the plain-clothes branch. At last he had been sent to the C.I.D. as a temporary aid, to see how he shaped, and though he had been in the force long enough to know that the life of a detective wasn't as glamorous as it was often painted he'd no idea that it could be as bad as this.

Stay there and watch the house, he had been told as a photograph of the absent Edwards was slipped into his hand. This is the man to look for. He might turn up and he might not, but the minute he does, we want to know; you'd better keep out of sight, too, because if he does come back we don't want to run any risk of frightening him.

That had been nearly an hour ago. It was another two at least before his relief was due and he was cold and cramped. He couldn't even stretch properly without running the risk of giving away his position, and the prospect of enjoying a smoke, with twigs poking in his face and tiny insects dropping down his back, was remote.

No one had gone into the house at all while he had been watching it other than a bloke and a hard-faced girl, who had seemed to be having some sort of argument. He watched them go in and settled back again. For all that the glitter looked to have worn off the girl a long time ago she was still passably pretty and there was nothing at all wrong with her figure. If he hadn't been practically engaged to Christine he could have used an hour alone with that bird. Spirited, too, from the looks of her and the way she was talking to the bloke.

Atkinson grinned. He liked spirited birds.

He was thinking of this and wondering how she might compare with Chris when he felt his eyes start to close. He jerked them open again, then rubbed them. Falling asleep on the job. There was only one thing worse than that, and that was punching the Super; either would be enough to get him kicked off the force. The trouble was that he'd had a late night last night, and now he was simply sitting here doing nothing.

It was enough to send anyone to sleep.

For something to do he slipped the photo of Edwards from his pocket and looked at it. A tough looking customer, he thought, and then a movement at the gate attracted his attention so he slipped the photo away again.

From where he was he couldn't see the gate properly because of a scrap car which was in front of the house, its tyres flat and one door missing, but there was no other spot where he could have hidden so well, and he could still see everyone who came up the path or left the house. From the sound of the person coming now he was moving very slowly.

Atkinson felt tension start to grow in his mind.

The footsteps came nearer and then he saw the man.

Edwards.

Even if he hadn't looked at the photo so recently, there would have been no doubt.

He was moving very slowly. Not suspiciously, but not rushing into anything either, almost as though he suspected that there might be cops around and he was taking no chances. Atkinson shivered as he looked at him; the photo had been only head and shoulders, and hadn't really given an impression of how massive the man was. There wouldn't be much percentage in tangling with him, though it might be something to tell Chris when he saw her that night. A lot of the things he did while he was on duty frightened her, and when she was frightened she had a habit of clinging very closely to him . . .

Edwards passed, staring at the bushes. Atkinson pressed himself back into them, anxious not to be seen, not because there might be trouble with Edwards if he was but because it might frighten him away.

He thought he saw Edwards hesitate, looking straight at him. He tensed, ready for trouble, but then Edwards walked on and went up the three steps which led to the house. When he was sure that there was no chance of Edwards turning round and seeing or hearing him, Atkinson moved, easing the cramp in his leg and reaching for the personal radio which was clipped to the inside of his jacket.

That was when he heard the scream and the gunshot.

At first he didn't realize what it was, but then he heard another scream. He remembered the girl and the bloke who'd gone in earlier. The screams could simply mean that he was sick of arguing with her and had decided to lay into her but there was no getting away from the fact that the sharp, flat crack he had heard had been made by a gun. He'd heard it often enough on the rifle range where he spent many of his leisure hours, and he couldn't be mistaken about it.

After hesitating for a couple of seconds he pressed down the switch on his personal radio and made a brief report before crawling out of the bushes and going to investigate.

★ ★ ★

Mark Edwards had an idea that there could be cops about as he came slowly up the path. There was no reason why there should be, he tried to tell himself, but he'd been in jail once and ever since then he'd been very careful, taking no chances, keeping out of trouble, listening to all the whispers on the criminal grapevine.

Even if he had to kill a cop to get away he wouldn't be caught again.

Since losing his gun at Hazel Manners' place he had had to get another from his usual source, and now his hand was in his pocket, resting lightly on the butt of it, as his eyes probed.

He saw no one.

Once he was inside the building he relaxed. It wasn't much of a place, but it was well off the usual criminal beat and the cops never gave it much attention. Most of the other tenants were young secretary birds who never gave any trouble; in the flat next to his was a married couple, trying to cut down on the amount they paid out in rent while they saved up for somewhere of their own.

He had nothing to do with any of them. As soon as he'd found that fifty-five thousand quid he was going to move some place else, and it wouldn't be in England.

He chuckled as he started to climb the stairs. What a dump this place was. It wasn't often that he felt like chuckling when he came in here. He tramped up the stairs to his flat, which was on the top floor, and noticed nothing wrong in the gloomy corridor.

He opened the door and went in.

Lee Packard turned from the far side of the room where he was looking in a drawer, and at the same moment Hazel Manners gave a little scream. Edwards had his gun out before he realized what he was doing.

Hazel screamed again as the bullet smacked into the wall about six inches from her head. Bits of plaster flaked down and landed on her hair as she flung herself on the floor, where Packard was already squirming his way across to Edwards.

'Get out of the damned way!' Edwards yelled.

He aimed the gun again but Hazel grabbed a small chair and tried to fling it at him. It didn't go anywhere near him, but it was enough to throw his aim out and let Packard get near enough to grab one of his legs. He pulled. Edwards kicked out with the other and Packard gave a wailing cry as the foot slammed into the side of his head. Dazed and sickened from the blow he squirmed on the floor, dimly aware that Edwards was jumping over him and that Hazel was shouting something in a thin, high pitched, monotonous voice.

'Shut up!' he yelled, his voice merely a croak in his dry throat, then he staggered to his feet. The room whirled around him but the dizzy feeling cleared very quickly and he saw Edwards vanishing out of the door. He had a sudden feeling that he was back at Hazel's, then he realized what was really happening, and ran after him.

'Be careful!' Hazel shouted.

Packard hardly heard her. Edwards was dodging about in the passage as if he didn't know which way to go; suddenly he turned away from the stairs and ran in the opposite direction.

When he got into the passage, Packard saw why. A tall, hefty looking bloke was hurrying towards them. He couldn't have been more obvious if he had had the word 'cop' written on his face in luminous paint. Packard hesitated then turned back and grabbed Hazel's hand, dragging her to her feet.

'The cops!' he hissed when she resisted, hardly realizing what he was doing.

That shook her. She hurried out after him. By now, the cop was near enough to block their path, and Packard, in a flat panic, didn't pause. He drove his fist into the cop's stomach and chopped at the back of his neck. As the cop fell, gasping and choking, they followed Edwards along the passage to a narrow doorway, wrenched it open and saw a flight of stairs which was obviously newer than the house and which must have been put in to comply with some fire regulation.

He started down them and stopped.

He could hear someone else. It could have been Edwards, but it didn't sound like him. Holding Hazel back with one hand, he leaned over the rail and peered down. He couldn't see very much but what he could make out was enough to start his heart thumping again, and make him feel even sicker than he had done when he had been kicked in the head.

Another couple of coppers were prowling about downstairs.

'Back up,' he told Hazel. 'We might be able to get to the front stairs again and out that way. The place is crawling with cops.'

'What about Edwards?' she demanded as they hurried up to the next floor.

'What about him? We've got other

worries. The cops couldn't touch us before but now that they've heard that gun they won't let it go until they find out what's happening. And I punched that one. I'm not letting them get hold of me.'

They reached the next passage. There was no one in sight here and they ran along it. When they came to the end they slowed and Packard peered round on to the stairs. There was no one in sight but as he stepped out, pulling Hazel after him, she suddenly said: 'There's someone coming up!'

The note of panic in her voice was unusual. He turned to look at her frightened, strained face, then she broke free from him and ran back along the passage. He would have gone after her but just then there was a yell from the direction of the stairs and he saw someone coming towards him.

It was the cop he had hit.

There was no time to work out a proper plan. It would have been stupid to run after Hazel and perhaps give away the fact that she was there; all he could do was go up the remaining stairs.

They led into a small, square room. It was empty and dusty, and the only other way out was through a tiny window. Packard hurried over to it. Even if it had been big enough to get out of he couldn't have managed to get down to the ground; it was too far to jump, and there were no pipes or gutters handy.

Panic stricken now, he stood in the room while the clumping sound of the cop's feet came nearer and nearer.

★　★　★

P.C. Atkinson smiled. This wasn't as boring now, and it was almost worth having crouched in those bushes for so long. He knew that the man he was chasing wasn't Edwards but he had no idea who he was; all he knew was that he could still feel the pain in his stomach where he had been hit, and that in itself gave him a savage feeling. He was going to arrest this character, gun or no gun, and if he got hurt while he was being taken down the stairs, that was his own fault. He would have brought it on himself while resisting arrest, and no one would be able to prove otherwise.

And then tonight he was looking forward to telling Christine how he had caught a gunman. He could see the look in her eyes now, the soft, loving expression, mingled with the instinctive horror of the dangers which her husband-to-be had to face.

In a way, he almost hoped that no one else would come.

He didn't know the layout of the house too well, but he had had a look round before taking up his post in the bushes, and one of the things he had found out was that both staircases were dead ends. He knew that the man was in that tiny room, and that there was no way out for him. The proper thing to do was wait here until help came, but he couldn't resist having a go himself.

Not after that thump in the stomach.

He moved nearer to the door, treading softly so that there would be no warning of his approach. He was so intent on that, listening for any sound from the room, that he never heard the person coming up behind him. The first he knew about that was when his head seemed to split open. He heard himself grunt with the pain, then he pitched forward and lay still.

13

Lee Packard was at the small window again, wishing that he'd never come in here and trying to find a way of getting down the walls outside. Too far away for him to have any hope of reaching them from here were the drainpipes, twisting their way to the ground, providing ample foot and hand holds for anyone shinning down. If the window in the room had been just a few feet further along he could easily have got out, but from here there was no hope. It was almost like being in a cell, and his lips twisted savagely as he realized that that was where he was likely to end up.

And all because of Hazel and her damned fifty-five thousand quid.

She wasn't here now. She wasn't trapped, the cops weren't going to get her.

The door opened and he whirled, his

fists bunching, ready to make a last attempt to fight his way out. As he started forward, the sight of Edwards and the gun brought him up short.

He ran his tongue over his lips.

'The cop — '

'The cop won't give any trouble,' Edwards said. 'It's you I'm worried about.'

'Now listen — '

'Come on,' Edwards said impatiently. 'We haven't got time to stand here yapping. Do you want to get out or don't you?'

Packard didn't speak. He was breathing heavily, but the thumping of his heart was starting to return to normal. His mind was working more smoothly, too, and he could see that while there might be some trap in this and that Edwards might start something once they were out of the building, it was at least a way out and a better one than he could have made on his own.

'Are you going to stand there all day like a hunk of beef?' Edwards snarled. 'This is a way out, pal. If you don't want to take it I haven't got time to hang around.'

'Hazel — '

'Hazel's on her own,' Edwards said bluntly. 'I think she's got away but in any case there isn't time to look for her.'

Packard moved forward slowly. He almost expected that Edwards was in league with the cops and this was just a trick to get him out of the room, and the sight of the policeman sprawled at the top of the stairs startled him.

'You've killed him!' he breathed. 'Christ, what a fool you are! They won't let up after this and — '

'He isn't dead, he'll come round in about ten minutes, so don't worry about him. I'm not so stupid that I'd kill a cop.'

They hurried down the stairs, Edwards going first, his eyes darting from side to side. No one at all was about. They reached the bottom and the entrance hall was clear.

'We might make it yet,' Edwards said.

'It can't be soon enough for me.'

They crossed the hall, their footsteps echoing, and stepped out into the drive.

Beyond the wrecked car they could see Packard's, still where he had left it, but with a police car drawn up in front of it. The blue light was still flashing, throwing an eerie glow over everything, but there were no cops near it.

'That your car?'

Packard nodded.

'They've hemmed you in pretty tight but you'll get out. Want me to drive?'

Packard nodded again and Edwards's lip curled slightly. They hurried into the street and jumped into the car. As Packard slammed his door and Edwards started the engine they heard a frantic shouting, and a moment later Hazel came running out of the front door. A cop was behind her, but it didn't look as though he was going to make it. Packard swung open the rear door. Edwards jumped out, leaving the engine running, and raised his gun.

Hazel was watching Packard. She hadn't seen Edwards and she ran on. The cop saw him and the gun and hesitated. With a final sprint she flung herself into the car, just as Edwards put two bullets into the police car's tyres. He swung round, scrambled into the driving seat and reversed with a jerk that almost sent Hazel on to the floor. He rammed in bottom gear, swung out and round the police car, and roared down the street.

That sound of Hazel as she gulped for breath came clearly over the noise of the engine.

As they got to the corner of the street they heard a blast from the police car's siren, but with two punctured tyres there was nothing they could do. Edwards was grinning as he turned the corner, narrowly missing a car which was turning in the opposite direction, heading for the house.

'See that?' Packard said when they were safely past. 'That's the big-shot in charge of the case, Superintendent Martin. He got here too late, didn't he?'

He chuckled with nervous reaction and Edwards moved his lips in something that might have been a smile. It was only then that Packard realized there could be more danger now than there would ever be from the cops.

* ★ ★

Back at the house, Martin stopped the car and jumped out. The Divisional Superintendent was with him and he frowned when he saw that none of his men were about.

'I wonder — ' he began, then stopped as a man came out of the house and down the steps, hurrying towards them.

'Where are they?' Martin demanded.

'They've got away, sir,' the man, Sergeant Price, said. 'You must have met them as you turned into the street. I gave you a blast on the siren hoping that you might realize what was going on.'

'Why couldn't you follow — ' the Divisional man, Superintendent Watson, said, then stopped when he saw the two flat tyres on the patrol car. 'When was that done?'

'There were three of them, sir,' Price said. 'Two men and a girl. I nearly got the girl but she managed to get into their car. One of the blokes shot up the tyres on ours and we hadn't a chance of following them.'

Martin looked as if he were about to say something, then he saw another man come out of the building. This was a constable who had been with Price in the car, and he looked white and shocked.

'What's the matter?' Watson demanded. 'And where's Atkinson? He was supposed to be watching in case Edwards came back.'

'He's upstairs, sir,' the constable blurted. 'I think we ought to get him to hospital. I was just going to radio — '

'What's wrong with him?' Watson broke in, alarm sharpening his voice, as Price turned to the immobile squad car and began to put in a call for an ambulance.

Quickly, the constable described what he had seen and how he had found Atkinson unconscious at the top of the stairs.

'I don't think he's seriously hurt, sir,' he finished, 'but he's certainly had a good crack over the head.'

'Recognize any of the men?' Martin asked.

He shook his head.

'I'd know them if I saw them again,' he

said, 'but I couldn't put names to them.'

'All right,' Martin said, and turned to Watson, as Price finished making his call. 'We might as well have a look round Edwards' place now that we're here.'

★　★　★

They found hardly anything in Edwards' flat, and certainly nothing to show that he was connected with the Wiggin Street bank robbery.

All they found was the bullet which Edwards had fired and which had hit the wall. The bullet was taken away for examination, but the only clear thing that came out was that it had been fired from a gun different to the one which had been used in the robbery and the killing of Terry Stevenson.

14

Edwards drove swiftly and well. He didn't speak during the journey, though from time to time he glanced sideways at Packard, and an amused smile came on his lips. Packard stared woodenly at him, wanting to speak, to ask Edwards what the hell he thought he was playing at, what he was going to do, but at the last minute thoughts of Edwards' possible reaction always stopped him.

Basically, he was afraid; he thought that Edwards would be sure to kill him now, and that it had been a mistake ever to go to his flat, even though they had phoned him twice and there had been no answer. It had seemed safe enough then, but it went to show that you could never tell.

And why had Edwards run from his own flat?

Agreed, the cops were there, but it still didn't make sense. All that Edwards would have to do was deny that he knew anything about it, and though there might have been some sticky moments he could probably have got away with it, because there would be no proof of anything Packard said, and the cops would have assumed that he was merely trying to confuse the issue now that he'd been caught.

So it followed that Edwards was up to something.

But what?

There was a lot to talk about as far as Packard was concerned, but he wondered whether he'd ever hear any of the answers to his questions. For all he knew the next half hour could see both him and Hazel dead. He shuddered, then realized that the car was slowing down and that they were outside Hazel's flat.

Edwards stopped the engine by the simple method of letting it stall with the car in gear, then he put it into neutral and pulled on the handbrake with a harsh, grating sound as the ratchet clicked; it seemed to Packard that if his nerves were plucked they'd make a noise like that, too.

'What's on your mind, Edwards?' Hazel

said, abruptly and hoarsely.

Edwards grinned.

'What makes you think there's anything on my mind?'

'From the look on your face you might be going to kill us.'

'I couldn't care less about you, baby,' Edwards declared. 'If I'd wanted to kill Packard I could have done it as easily back there as anywhere else.'

'With the cops there?' Packard sneered.

'I'd have got out. Don't worry about that.'

'You live there — ' Hazel began.

'I'm not that attached to the place. There are plenty of other flats I can rent.'

She saw that a nerve in the side of his face was twitching. There was a thin film of sweat on his forehead, too, but those were the only signs that he had been at all shaken by what had happened.

'Suppose we go up to your place?' he went on, 'I don't like sitting in cars in the street. It makes you too noticeable, especially in a crate like this. Why don't you get yourself something that doesn't

154

look as though it came out of a scrapyard, Packard?'

He sneered the last word and grinned at the expression which came on Packard's face.

Packard said nothing.

They got out of the car and went up to the flat, still without speaking; Hazel opened the door, and Edwards barged in ahead of everyone.

'Don't mind me,' Hazel said sharply, as she was pushed to one side.

'I wouldn't mind you for an hour alone in the back of that heap of Packard's,' he said, laughing and sprawling in one of the chairs. 'Don't be so touchy, sister, I'm here to help you.'

'When I want help from people like you I'll shoot myself first.'

She looked at Packard who sat down on the settee, stared at Edwards and said:

'All right, quit the smart talk and tell us what you're after. You won't get it, and when you've finished you can clear out.'

Edwards draped one leg over the arm of his chair. Hazel crossed to the cabinet of drinks and poured out three stiff whiskies; she looked as if she would have liked to ram Edwards' down his throat while it was still in the glass, but he had his gun tucked into his pocket and she was wary of starting trouble.

He took the glass from her and gulped down the drink, smacking his lips.

'I needed that, baby,' he told her. 'You make a good drink.'

'What do you want?' Packard insisted.

'What were you doing at my place?'

Packard hesitated, and Edwards waved his arm.

'All right,' he said, 'you don't want to tell me so I'll tell you. You think that I killed Georgina Lewis and you were hoping you'd find some proof.'

'Didn't you?' Hazel demanded.

'Look at it this way,' Edwards said easily, almost as if he was trying to sell them something. 'She knows where she could have put her hands on fifty-five thousand quid, and if I'd got hold of her I'd have made her tell me that. I'm not so stupid that I'd kill her just because I didn't like her face. Do I look as if I'm mad?'

Packard opened his mouth to say something but before he could speak Hazel said:

'It could have been an accident.'

'I don't have accidents like that.'

'She could have told you where it was, and then you killed her.'

'You're assuming I'm stupid again,' Edwards said. 'If she'd told me where all that money was do you think I'd have gone back to that crummy flat?' He paused. 'Would you have gone back there if you'd had fifty-five thousand quid? I didn't kill her and I don't know where the stuff is.'

'We worked it out like this,' Packard said. 'You killed her. Because of that, the cops are interested, obviously, and as soon as they started checking into her movements they could have found out that she was at my place.'

'Was she?'

'Last night when you were looking for her,' Packard said with a faint grin. 'She must have broken in while you were following me.'

'Then how come she was killed at her

own flat? That's the place where she'd expect to find me looking for her.'

'I know,' Packard said. 'What worried me is that someone could have told the cops that they'd seen her around my place. I blundered in right after the body had been found, and if they do discover she was at my flat it'll make nonsense of the story I told them. In any case, they've got my name and address now and if they don't find out anything else they'll start investigating me.'

'And that'll turn up a lot of stuff you'd rather keep hidden?'

Packard nodded.

'The other thing we thought,' he said, 'is that if you'd killed her you'd have the money by now, and you might have felt like tipping off the cops that it was me who'd done it.'

'So you went round to my flat trying to find out what I was up to?'

'Yeah. We phoned you, to make sure you were out. There was no answer and no reply when we knocked so we reckoned that it was safe.'

'Wrong, weren't you?' Edwards grinned

at Hazel, whose face was expressionless.

She still hadn't recovered properly from the shock of what had happened at Edwards' place. It had been so different from what she'd expected, from the simple operation it had sounded as Packard had described it. When they had got there he had knocked on the door as a final check, then taken a small bunch of keys from his pocket, each key made from twisted wire.

'One of these beauties will open it,' he'd said confidently, separating a few from the main bunch.

Hazel had watched. She had seen Packard open doors with these keys before, but it still fascinated her. Once, he had startled her by breaking into her own flat in exactly a minute and a half when she had challenged him to show her how quickly he could do it; now, she kept watch while he twisted his skeleton keys about in the lock. After a minute or two he'd given a satisfied grunt and the door had swung open.

They'd gone in and searched, but found nothing.

Fifteen minutes later, Edwards had arrived . . .

'Why did you get us out of there?' she asked abruptly. 'Wouldn't it have been simpler to have turned us over to the cops and have done with it?'

'What a lovely tale you could have told them, though,' Edwards said. 'Let's go into it, shall we? First of all there was that shot. It was a mistake on my part, but the cops would still have wanted an explanation for it, and when they hadn't found a gun on you it would have thrown it right back to me. Then I guessed that you'd think I killed Georgina. I didn't, but there was no point in having you give the cops ideas like that, and it was simpler to get you out. I won't be going back there. The cops are welcome to what's left.'

'Tell me,' Packard said, 'if you didn't kill Georgina, how did you know she was dead?'

There was a pause. Hazel ran her tongue over her lips, and Edwards looked from one to the other of them with a sneering expression on his face.

'Smart, aren't you, Packard?' he said

thoughtfully. 'Why don't you join the cops? They're looking out for bright young men like you.'

'Leave the funnies out of it,' Packard snarled, 'and just answer the questions.'

'I found out by accident,' Edwards said smoothly. 'After you and me had that bit of trouble here I walked round for a while trying to work things out, and getting a new gun from a mate of mine, and then I went into a café. They had the local radio on, and there was an announcement on the news. That's all there is to it.'

Packard didn't relax, but it was obvious that he'd become more thoughtful. At first, there had been no doubt in his mind that Edwards was the killer, but now he wasn't so sure. It wasn't reasonable to assume that he would have killed her without finding out where the money was, yet if he knew that, why was he hanging round here? That didn't make sense either, and Packard found himself with all his neat theories turned upside down.

'Does it make sense or doesn't it?' Edwards demanded.

'I suppose it does,' Packard replied, gulping his whisky.

'Then see if this makes as much sense. The cops are involved now that someone's been killed, and they may have found out by now that Georgina's death is tied in with the Wiggin Street robbery. If they're sniffing around and we're fighting each other neither of us is going to get very far and the cops are going to get all the pickings. Right?'

'I can see what you're getting at,' Hazel said unexpectedly, when Packard hesitated. 'You think that we should join forces against the cops?'

'Not so much against them as against the original gang. Don't forget that they're still around somewhere, and if the three of us are fighting against each other as well, we aren't going to get anywhere.'

'But — ' Packard began.

'Can't you make Packard see that?' Edwards said to Hazel. 'It's the only thing to do.'

'Perhaps I can see it already,' Packard said. 'More to the point is what do you intend to do now, if we agree to work with you?'

'We want to know where the money is,' Edwards said. 'We were all relying on Georgina telling us, but that's a bit of a dead end now.'

'In more ways than one. It only goes to show why she was killed.' Packard stared at him, then set down his empty glass. 'Where do we go from here?'

'We go to see a guy named Cummins,' Edwards said. 'She used to work for him. She could have said something to him before she ran away, and he's probably the best hope now. I've got another line out, too, trying to find out who worked with Terry Stevenson on the Wiggin Street job, but I haven't had anything from it yet. I'll let you know as soon as there's anything I can tell you.'

Packard nodded.

Hazel said: 'There's only one thing to be worked out before we start. When we get this money, how are we going to split it?'

Edwards turned to stare at her and there was a tense silence in the room.

15

'Look,' Edwards said, 'there's enough to argue about and discuss, without bringing that into it. Why don't we leave it until we've got some money to share out? We might never find it if all we're going to do is sit here and argue.'

'I'd still like to know what you've got in mind,' she insisted.

'If you knew what was in his mind you'd never speak to him again,' Packard said. 'He's right, Hazel, we've been sitting here talking for too long.'

Hazel didn't say anything. The old glitter was back in her eyes and Packard realized that until now she hadn't really recovered from the near miss of being caught back at the flat. Now that she had and was starting to pick holes in the plan Edwards had put forward, anything could happen. He thought that she might start arguing with him properly, which could only end in Edwards getting out his gun again, and he was relieved when she didn't say anything else.

There was another silence.

'I just thought I'd mention it,' she said, 'so that you can keep it in mind while you're seeing this character Cummins.'

'I'll keep it in mind,' he said mildly.

'The only other thing is how do we know you'll be straight with us?' Packard asked.

'You'll have to trust me. I wouldn't have got you out of that jam just to double-cross you. I'd have let you stew.'

'All right,' Packard said. 'I'll phone you tonight and see how much further you've got. Just watch that you don't try any funny business.'

'I won't,' Edwards said. He grinned at him, winked at Hazel and went out, shutting the door softly.

Packard looked at Hazel, then at the skull which was staring sightlessly at him.

'I don't like him,' he said.

'Neither do I. He's about as safe as a boxful of cobras but we had no choice. What happened after we got split up at his place?'

He explained about the cop and the small room and the way Edwards had got him out of it.

'No chance of that cop thinking you're the one who slugged him, is there?'

'I shouldn't think so. I wasn't even in sight when it happened and he must have known that I couldn't have got out of that room and come up behind him.'

'So that's not his game. He was right about it being good for him to get us out of there, but I can't see why he should go to all this trouble about getting us to work with him.'

Packard shook his head.

'Me neither. Perhaps the thought of the gang lurking around is worrying him. He might think he stands to get knocked off if he goes on much longer. Remember, they don't know a thing about us and we should be reasonably safe.'

'I'm still not sure. He's up to something but God knows what. We'll have to wait and see.'

It was a little after half past three when Packard eventually left to go back home. He drove carefully, not quite sure how clearly the police had seen him at Edwards', and whether or not they would know who he was. He saw nothing suspicious on the way and there were no cops lurking about outside the house. He ran quickly up the stairs, opened the door of his flat and went in. A blow scythed down at his head, and he had a dim glimpse of a man jumping through the open door.

* * *

'It's nothing to do with me,' Edwards said half an hour later when Packard phoned him at the hotel where he was staying. 'Why should I want to do something like that? If I'd wanted to beat you over the head there are plenty of easier ways I could have used.'

'So who was it then?'

'Who killed Georgina?' Edwards countered.

'But they've never heard of me, or Hazel,' Packard said. 'How would they know to come and beat me up?'

Edwards laughed softly.

'Don't you believe it,' he said. 'I reckon that this gang know a lot more than any of us think. Do you still need proof that we've got to work together against them if we're going to have any chance of getting this money?'

*   *   *

On the following afternoon, everything was quiet in Martin's office. The results of the tests on the bullet which had been fired at Edwards' had come in that morning; the gun was certainly not the one which had been used in the robbery, or the murder of Terry Stevenson, and it wasn't even one which was known to the police from something else. Martin had had great hopes of that bullet, but now he felt that he was back where he'd started. The only hope was that Fingerprints would come up with something; they had gone over the flat thoroughly and the prints which had shown up were being checked now against the central files.

It had been a long job taking them; it would take just as long to check each one and find out who the other people had been.

When they knew that, they might be able to clear up another puzzling factor.

All of them had got away in the same car, which suggested that they were friends of Edwards. There was nothing wrong in that, but if it was so, why had the shots been fired?

'Let's go over what we've got,' he said to Brady, 'and see if we can sort out anything from it.'

'There isn't much to go over, is there?' Brady asked, a gloomy expression on his normally cheerful face. 'How's that chap who was attacked at Edwards' place?'

'Atkinson? Better than we hoped,' Martin said. 'He'll be off duty for a week or so, but he should be fine after that. If he'd been hit a little harder, his skull would have been smashed open, no doubt about that. Whoever hit him wasn't in any mood for playing about.'

'I wonder what they stand to gain?' Brady said. 'Are you sure that it's to do with this bank robbery?'

'Let's start at the beginning. It might

pull things together. A girl named Georgina Lewis was killed. From all accounts she was a loose piece but there was no reason as far as we can see why anyone should want to stick a knife in her back. People who know her and live in the same building, and her employer, Steven Cummins, say that she's been away about a week. We also know that she was friendly with a bloke called Stevenson who was shot the other night.'

'That's straighforward enough,' Brady commented.

Martin nodded.

'Now let's go back about a month,' he went on. 'One Monday round about then there was a bank robbery in Wiggin Street. A man who got in the way of the raiders when they were escaping had his head smashed in with an iron bar, and was killed. A couple of shots were fired. They didn't hit anyone and we were able to dig one of the bullets out of the bank door, and one out of a shop window frame across the road. The bullets and the one which killed Terry Stevenson match, and some of the money was found in his rooms, so that ties all this up with the bank robbery. Fifty-five thousand pounds was stolen then, and the money Stevenson had is the only part of it that's come to light.'

'With that as a motive they won't stop at anything,' Brady said.

Martin leaned back. That was what he was afraid of: that the killing and the violence which they had seen so far was merely a start. There was no telling how many other people were involved; the Wiggin Street job was the work of a gang, but there was no way of knowing whether it was an established one or one which had been formed specially for the purpose.

He opened a folder on his desk and began to turn over a pile of reports. There were dozens of them, all concerning the Wiggin Street job.

'Not a clue,' he said. 'All these words and all these statements, and there isn't a thing which points anywhere. Not a thing.'

'Think it could be any of the big boys?' Brady asked. 'You know, the ones we've heard about but can't quite pin anything on.'

Martin shook his head.

'Somehow I don't think so. The impression I get from reading all this stuff is that it was a very amateurish affair, and any of the big gangs could have pulled it much better. I think we'll find it was just a few hoodlums who got together to rob the bank and now they're falling out over the division of the loot. That would explain why none of it's turned up yet, and maybe the shots that were fired at Edwards' flat.'

He broke off as there came a tap on the door.

'Come in,' Brady called, but the door was already opening to admit a dark, well-built man. He had some papers in his hand and he laid them on Martin's desk before dropping into the spare chair and pushing a loose lock of hair out of his eyes.

'What are those?' Martin demanded.

'Some reports on those fingerprints at Edwards',' the man said. 'Nothing very interesting about them really.'

Martin waited. He had known Frank Thesser for a long time and knew that it was no use trying to hurry him up. Whatever he had to say would be said in his own time, and attempts to make him get it over a bit faster would only confuse things and slow them down even more.

'Come on, Frankie boy,' Brady said. 'What have you got for us?'

Martin gave him a warning glance, leaned back and took out his pipe. As he was filling it Thesser said:

'Most of the prints belong to Edwards. There are some others which match with a lot at Georgina's place and which are obviously hers. And there's this.'

He used his forefinger to separate one of the papers from the rest.

'That's a photograph of a palm print which we found by the door of Edwards' flat,' he said. 'There was only the one and the funny thing is that it was much fresher than any of the others. The bloke who left it there has a record.'

'Has he indeed!' Martin exclaimed, jerking upright and forgetting his pipe, which was refusing to light. 'Who is he?'

'Chap named Lee Packard. He was pulled in about five years ago for dipping. That's all the record he's got.'

Martin pulled the photo of the print towards him. It was slightly over life-size and though he wasn't an expert on fingerprints it was easy to see that it was similar to the one of Packard's which was mounted alongside it; Thesser had drawn neat arrows to show each point where the two matched, and there was no doubt at all they were the same.

Thesser stood up.

'That help you, Don?'

'You don't know how much,' Martin said. 'Thanks a lot, Frank, this will come in really useful.'

'Any time,' Thesser said. 'Be seeing you, I've a lot to do.' He went out, and as the door closed behind him Brady said:

'Isn't Packard the character who was at Georgina's and who said he was a friend of hers?'

'And didn't know too much about her?' He grinned. 'That's the one. So he's been at Edwards' recently, has he?'

He reached out for the phone and

asked for Superintendent Watson. When he was through he said:

'Tom, have you got descriptions from your chaps of those men who were at Edwards' yesterday?'

'They're in front of me now,' Watson said. 'I've just had them typed out. What's on?'

Martin described Packard and Watson listened in silence. When the description finished he said:

'There's one of them who could fit in with that. No one got a very clear view of him and he wasn't the one with the gun, that's definite, but he could well have been there.'

'His prints have been found in Edwards' flat,' Martin explained. 'He's got a record otherwise we wouldn't have known who he was.'

'Where does he live?'

'Don't worry, he's not on your ground. I'll get on to Sid Newton and see what he knows.'

He hung up and was soon speaking to Newton, who was in charge of the Division in which Packard's home lay. He explained something of what he wanted, without going into too much detail, and asked what they knew of Packard at the Division.

'Officially, I don't think there's much,' Newton said, after thinking for a moment. 'He's a small, snub-nosed chap with very long fingers if it's the one I'm thinking of.'

'That's him.'

'Just a minute. Let me get my black book out, see if there's anything in there.' There was a clatter of a phone being laid on the desk and then just the humming of the line.

Brady raised his eyebrows in enquiry.

'Nothing official,' Martin said. 'If he's kept out of trouble since that conviction he could have been doing anything and we wouldn't know about it. Going off his record he seems a bit small-time to be involved in something like that Wiggin Street do, but you can never tell.'

He paused, thinking he could hear Newton coming back, but there was nothing.

'He's just looking in the book where he makes his own notes of things he suspects but can't prove,' Martin went on. 'We'll see what turns up.'

He waited for another half-minute and then Newton was back.

'Don,' he said, 'there's nothing specific against him but we think that he's still working the dip trade around the West End. He's being very clever about it, though, and there's nothing we can prove.'

'Think he'd go in for a bank robbery, say the Wiggin Street job?'

'Not off this lot,' Newton said. 'Can't be sure of it, but I'd say that it's not very likely.'

'Okay, Sid, thanks, I'll come back to you if I want anything more.' He hung up, and told Brady the result.

'Not very helpful, is it?' Brady said. 'Are we going to pull him in?'

'We could do and charge him with assaulting Atkinson,' Martin said. 'It looks as though he was the one that punched him in the stomach, even if he couldn't have hit him over the head. I'd do that, but I think we'd be rushing things if we did.'

'How come?'

Martin sat back thoughtfully, running over in his mind the various alternatives.

'I think it might be better to keep an eye on him,' he said eventually and see who he's meeting, who his friends are, things like that. Once we get a line on him we might find someone connected with him who's more likely to have been involved in the Wiggin Street job.'

'Talking of Packard's friends, I wonder where Edwards has gone now? And who the girl was?'

Martin shrugged.

'They're only two of the questions I want answering.' He reached out as the phone bell rang, and scooped up the receiver. 'Martin.'

'Hello, Don,' a voice said. 'Hadleigh here. They tell me you're looking for a character named Mark Edwards.'

'Have you got him there?' Martin demanded urgently, and there was a pause during which the tension seemed to become unbearable.

16

While Martin and Brady were at Scotland Yard, going through the reports which had been amassed on the Wiggin Street robbery, trying to fit them in with the latest events, and, later, talking to Chief Inspector Charles Hadleigh, Hazel Manners was at home in her flat. Packard wasn't there for once; he was in his own home, and she had become so used to seeing him in the chair across from her that the place looked strangely empty without him.

She was determined to find that money.

Fifty-five thousand pounds was more than she had ever dreamed of before, and she was certain that when it was found Mark Edwards wasn't going to get a penny, though it was a good idea to let him think that she and Packard had teamed up with him. He was nothing to her. But for the fact that he'd returned to his flat and caught them there they'd never have had anything to do with him, and Hazel didn't see why they should share the money with him now; Georgina had been her friend, not his, and if anyone was going to have that money it should be her, Hazel Manners, and Lee.

Definitely not Edwards.

He might even have killed her, though she didn't really think so now; his arguments against it were too persuasive, and there was no reason why he should have done. Not only that, but if he knew where the money was, why was he still hanging around, making a nuisance of himself? Unless he was working some risky plan of his own to set them up as fall-guys for the cops, there was no reason, and Hazel was inclined to think that he had no more idea where the stuff was than she had.

Of all the people who could have killed Georgina, the original gang, who must have realized that she was a threat to them, were most likely, but there was another prospect which frightened her even more than the thought of tangling with people like that.

Packard could have done it.

At first, that idea hadn't entered her head, because he had told her how he'd got home to find Georgina missing, gone to her flat and been told by the cops that she'd been murdered. That had sounded fine and she'd been too busy worrying about the implications of it all to wonder if things had really happened that way.

Suppose they hadn't?

Suppose he'd found her gone from his place, but she'd still been alive when he'd followed her. There could have been an argument over something, he could have killed her and then gone back later simply to see what the cops were doing and what they'd found out. It would have been risky, but probably not as risky as being left in the dark.

When she saw him again she was going to have to ask him. No matter what the answer was, she would have to know; until then she would have no peace of mind, no freedom from the thought that there could be another tangle to this situation, one which she hadn't figured but which could affect her more than anything else had done.

And Packard would tell her, that was certain. Even if he didn't want to at first, she was sure that she'd be able to get it out of him one way or another and find out the truth; once she knew that, she would be better able to make her own plans, and decide what she was going to do.

Either way, there was nothing on her. The cops couldn't frighten her, no matter what they said or did, because she hadn't done a thing wrong. At least, there was nothing they could prove, which came to the same thing. They couldn't even show definitely that she'd been the girl at Edwards' flat, though they'd probably have a good enough try at getting her to admit it if they ever got near her.

She glanced at the clock.

It was half past nine.

At ten, she'd put on the television news; it wasn't something she normally did, but there might be new developments in the case and if there were she wanted to know about them. After that she'd go to bed, then in the morning when Packard came round she'd see what he had to say. The thoughts of asking him worried her a little, but it was a long time off yet, and she tried to put it out of her mind.

A slight sound in the passage outside made her look towards the door.

There was nothing, as far as she knew. Probably it was one of the two old bags living upstairs messing at something or other.

She wouldn't be sorry to get this fifty-five thousand quid, just so she could get out of this dump. Modelling wasn't a bad way of bringing in the weekly money, but she was getting a fraction too old for that now, and within a year or so she'd be finished entirely. She giggled suddenly. Too old, at twenty-eight! Things were coming to something when that happened. The real explanation, she tried to tell herself, wasn't that she was losing her youthful looks but that the public was tiring of the same old faces and wanted someone new. Well, they were welcome. When she had fifty-five thousand quid she wouldn't be prancing around in front of cameras, there was nothing surer than that.

But first she had to get the money.

That was going to be the difficult part. That, and taking it off Edwards, who seemed to know more about what he was doing than either she or Packard did. Not for the first time she wondered why he had teamed up with them and what was in his mind. Was it really that he was afraid they would yap to the cops, or that he feared trouble from the original gang, or was there some other reason?

There was no way of knowing.

All she could do was wait and see, and by then it might be too late.

She heard the sound in the passage again, and frowned. This time it had been louder and there was no mistaking the fact that it was almost outside her front door, a scratching sound, and a soft murmuring of voices. Before she could do anything about it, there was a sharp ring at the bell.

With no thought of danger in her mind

she stood up and went to answer the door.

★　★　★

Lee Packard heard the sharp ring of the phone bell. He was sitting in the chair half asleep at the time, and at first he wasn't going to answer it. Settling himself more comfortably in the chair he listened to the ringing for what seemed a long time; instead of cutting off as he'd expected, the sound went on and on.

Presently, irritated by the constant noise, he stood up and crossed to the phone. Probably it was some kid with a wrong number. If it was, and he'd been disturbed just for that, he'd make them think twice next time.

He grabbed the receiver.

'Hello!' he snarled into it.

'Mr Packard?'

'Well?'

The voice was soft at first, in sharp contrast to Packard's shout; next time it spoke, it was a little louder, and the words were very clear.

185

'When do you expect to see Hazel Manners again, Mr Packard?' it asked.

'Tomorrow morning,' he answered, so surprised that he didn't even ask who was calling or what business it was of theirs when he saw her.

'What makes you so sure?' the voice said, and the line went dead.

Packard stared stupidly at the receiver, then replaced it slowly. Kids. It must be. They could have found out his name easily enough, and someone had probably told them that he was going around with Hazel, someone who would think a call like that would be a huge joke. It was a trick to worry him, that was all, and they'd have someone standing outside her door, listening for the phone, gleeful when it rang because they'd know it was him checking up.

Well he wasn't going to.

He settled back in the chair again. He should have switched on the news at ten o'clock, he thought, and seen whether or not there was anything new about the murder, but it hadn't occurred to him. Hazel might know; she was likely to have done that, and he could ask her tomorrow.

Tomorrow.

What made him so sure he was going to see her tomorrow morning?

He shook himself, angry now because that soft, clear voice had rattled him. He tried to forget it, but it kept coming back, tightening his nerves and making sure that he was unable to relax into the comfortable stupor which he'd fallen into earlier.

The phone bell rang again.

He jumped up, crossed over to it and snatched the receiver off the prongs.

'Mr Packard?' It was a different voice this time, with a harsher tone than before. 'When do you expect to see Hazel Manners again?'

'Tomorrow morning.'

'What makes you so sure?'

He banged down the receiver, hesitated for a moment then picked it up again and dialled Hazel's number, surprised to find that his hands were trembling. It rang for a long time. He cut himself off, then tried again, letting it ring for nearly five minutes before giving up.

What made him so sure . . .

That second call hadn't sounded like a child, and now that there was no answer from Hazel's number it was starting to be worrying. He wondered what was going on, why anyone should want to do anything like this, and where Hazel could be. She might be working, of course; he hadn't thought of that until now, but on the other hand she'd said nothing to him about a modelling job tonight, and with the situation as it was he didn't think she'd have taken one that cropped up suddenly.

Mark Edwards.

It could be some trick of his, of course. He'd never really believed that story he'd tried to feed them about working together. As far as Packard was concerned that was so much rubbish, and all that Edwards was really waiting for was a chance to get them in bad with the cops so that he could double-cross them. That was almost certain to be his basic plan, and he could have started already. There'd been no word from him since he'd gone to see Steven Cummins yesterday, where Georgina had worked, and this could be his next move.

Stabbing at the dial now, he dialled Edwards' number.

There was no answer from that, either.

He replaced the receiver and poured himself a drink. The best thing was to quit fooling about with the phone, go to Hazel's and see for himself what was going on. Even if she wasn't there he might find some clue as to where she'd gone. Perhaps there was some simple explanation involving one of her photographer friends, but if there wasn't then Edwards must have had a hand in it.

He stared at the phone, daring it to ring.

Another of those voices now would be more than he could take.

After a moment he turned away to get his coat before going round to Hazel's. While he was in the other room he heard the familiar shrilling start again, and he was half-way to the phone before he realized that the sound was actually from the door bell.

He opened the door.

He saw the cop he had seen at Georgina's, Chief Superintendent Martin.

'Good evening, Mr Packard,' Martin said, pleasantly enough. 'Could I come in and have a word with you for a few minutes?'

'I don't see why — '

Another figure stepped round the side of the door, and Martin broke in smoothly:

'You don't know Inspector Brady, do you? He's working with me, looking into the murder of Georgina Lewis.'

'What do you want?'

'We only want to ask you a few questions, that's all.'

He stepped forward, and Packard saw the hopelessness of trying to stop him from coming in. He fell back, then closed the door after them.

'Were you on your way out?' Martin enquired, gesturing towards the overcoat.

'I was going to see my girlfriend, if it's any business of yours,' Packard said viciously. He knew that he wasn't handling this well but the phone calls were still very fresh in his memory, and had rattled him more than he would be prepared to admit.

'You'd be surprised at what turns out to be business of mine,' Martin said. 'Better phone her and tell her you'll be late, because my questions might take some time to answer.'

Packard ran his tongue over his lips, glancing towards the phone, but not moving.

Martin watched him curiously. From what he now knew about Packard he could guess that he'd have no love for the cops, but he'd never have expected that a simple call, even at this time of the evening, would throw him into such an obvious panic. He wondered what was going on, and felt a slight tingle of excitement, as if he realized subconsciously that he was near the end of the case.

Slowly, Packard reached out for the phone.

It shrilled.

He started back as if it had reared up to bite him, and Brady winked at Martin then picked up the receiver himself.

'What makes you so sure, Mr Packard?' a voice said before he had time to speak, then chuckled softly.

'Hello!' Brady's voice was sharp but the phone was dead, and it was obvious that the caller had no idea that he hadn't been speaking to Packard.

He turned slowly, looking at Packard, whose face had gone white.

'Queer friends you have, Mr Packard,' he said. 'What does make you so sure? It sounds like some sort of riddle to me but I'll bet it isn't, is it?'

Packard looked as though he wasn't going to answer. He merely stared at the two policemen, then suddenly he backed against the wall, his eyes gleaming.

'It's Mark Edwards!' he cried. 'He's double-crossing me and he's killed Hazel! If anything's happened to her, he's the man you want.'

'Has anything happened to Hazel?' Martin demanded, not sure who they were talking about, but guessing she must be the girl who had been at Edwards'.

Packard nodded.

'When did you last see her?'

'I — ' Packard broke off. 'What has that got to do with you?'

'Just answer the question, Mr Packard. I've already told you, you'd be surprised what turns out to be my business.'

'I saw her this morning,' Packard said.

'And you're sure that Mark Edwards is involved in whatever has happened to her since then?'

'Sure? Of course I'm sure. He's been ringing me up all the evening, getting at me, trying to put my nerves on edge. He's got some idea in his mind and he's trying to soften me up for it now so that I'll be an easy mark for the rest of it. It won't work though, there's no danger of that.'

He broke off, as if he realized that he'd said too much, and there was a silence in the room. Brady opened his mouth as if to say something, but Martin gave him a warning glance.

Packard stared from one to the other of them. His eyes were still bright. He was breathing quickly, and his whole body was tense.

Martin took another step into the

room, his bulk seeming to fill it, and Packard's eyes became even rounder.

'Mr Packard,' Martin said, 'are you trying to tell me that you don't know Mark Edwards was murdered last night?'

17

'Murdered?' Packard demanded. 'Are you sure?'

'I've never seen anyone deader,' Martin declared briskly. 'I think you'd better sit down, Mr Packard, and tell me what you know about him.'

Packard nodded dully. He moved, walking backwards. The backs of his knees caught on the edge of the settee and he flopped down. Brady took out his notebook, moved round Martin, and settled himself at the table.

Martin didn't speak right away, remembering the message that had come in from Hadleigh. The body had been discovered an hour or two before that, shot in the head and dumped, probably from a car; from the details that were known there were no doubts that it was Edwards, and none that he had been killed the previous night. The Divisional Surgeon was very definite about that.

So he could have nothing to do with any phone calls to Packard, nor with anything that had happened to this girl, Hazel.

'Right,' he said. 'For a start I'd like you to tell me exactly who Hazel is.'

'My girlfriend.' There was defiance in Packard's voice, even though he realized it would do him no good in the end.

'What's her full name?'

'Hazel Manners.'

'She the girl who was with you when you went to Mark Edwards' flat yesterday?'

'She — ' Packard broke off. 'How did you know about that?'

Martin smiled faintly.

'Caught you on the hop there, didn't I? Now that we've established where you were yesterday afternoon you'd better tell me where you spent last night, from about seven o'clock.'

'I was with Hazel,' Packard said. 'You needn't try and pin any murders on me because it won't work.'

'I'm not trying to. I'm just having a little chat with you.'

He didn't add that he'd come round here specially to question Packard about the murder; there was no proof at all that he'd been involved in it, but its discovery put a different light on things and there was little point now in wasting time having him watched. He was definitely tied in with some of Edwards' rackets, and a few words with him might blow the whole thing open.

'Hazel will tell you that we spent the whole evening at her place,' Packard said.

'Where does she live?'

Packard gave him the address. Brady made a note of it, then glanced up.

'Talking of Hazel,' he said, 'didn't you mention something about a lot of phone calls? Was that queer one I took just now anything to do with it?'

'I don't know,' Packard said with a shrug, and a bland expression on his face. 'You didn't give me time to answer it, did you? If you hadn't hung up before I could get anywhere near the phone I might know better who it was.'

'You had plenty of time,' Brady said. 'From the way you started shouting afterwards I reckon you know plenty about it, but to make sure I'll tell you again what it was. All that was said was 'What makes you so sure, Mr Packard?' Nothing else, yet right away you started screaming about Mark Edwards. It looks funny to me.'

'There've been a couple of queer phone calls already tonight,' he said sullenly. 'I thought that was another of them, and it must be Edwards playing some stupid trick. If he's dead, it can't be, can it?'

'Why should he want to play tricks like that?' Martin asked.

Packard didn't answer.

Martin moved closer, and raised his voice.

'Listen, Packard, we already know too much about you for your own good. We know why you spend so much time at the Tower and on Oxford Street, we know all your little pickpocket tricks, so you'd better not get funny. There's also a question of assaulting a police constable.'

Packard's face went even whiter.

Slowly, they broke him down. He told them how he'd come home the other night and found Georgina in his flat. She was a friend of Hazel's he said, and Mark Edwards had been chasing her. He'd gone round to Edwards' flat, with Hazel, to see what he wanted, and there'd been trouble when Edwards had returned unexpectedly.

Martin listened in silence.

At the end, Packard stared at him; there was a hopeful expression in his eyes which made it fairly obvious that he hadn't told the whole truth and was hoping that his story had gone down well.

It was this more than any flaw in the story itself which put Martin on his guard.

'Had you ever seen Georgina before that?' he asked casually.

'No.'

'Odd that she turned up at your flat, isn't it? If it had been me instead of her I think I'd have run to someone I knew better.'

'Edwards was chasing her!' Packard cried. 'He saw her go to Hazel's so she couldn't stay there. Hazel sent her to me.' He broke off, and then his eyes widened;

not in fear this time but as if he'd just remembered something. 'Hazel!' he exclaimed. 'Where is she? There's those phone calls and no answer from her flat and — '

'When did the phone calls start?'

'About an hour ago. The one just after you'd arrived was the third.'

'Was it the same caller each time?'

Packard hesitated.

'I think so,' he said finally. 'He might have tried to disguise his voice one of the times.'

'Did he say anything on the other times that he didn't say to me?' Brady put in.

'He asked me when I expected to see Hazel again. When I told him tomorrow morning he asked me if I was sure.' Packard paused. 'Why are you just standing about?' he demanded. 'I always thought coppers were no good, but this proves it.'

'There's no point in making fools of ourselves by rushing off before we're ready,' Martin said. 'If this has been going on for an hour already we aren't going to lose much by spending five minutes getting the full facts. Have you a photograph of her?'

'I think so, I — ' Packard broke off. 'There's one in the other room.' He stood up and went to get it. When he came back he handed it to Martin, who smiled faintly.

'So she did go with you to see Edwards.'

'What if she did?'

'That copper's still in hospital after that little do,' Martin reminded him.

'That's nothing to do with me. I didn't hit no copper, at least not enough to put him in hospital.'

'Leave it for now,' Martin said, 'and tell me what happened afterwards. If you were so anxious to defend Georgina against Edwards why did you team up to get away? It wasn't because you were all so frightened of the police that you wanted to hold each other's hands, was it?' He was still probing, still looking for the weakness which must lie somewhere in what Packard had said. 'And how did Georgina get from your flat to hers when she was killed?'

'She went for some clothes,' Packard said.

Martin raised his eyebrows.

'With Edwards after her I'd have thought that was the last thing she would have done, once she'd found a safe hiding place.'

Packard shrugged.

Martin said: 'More important than that, why did you lie to me when you came to the flat after her?'

Packard didn't answer that. To do so would have involved explaining about the money, and as long as the cops knew nothing about that —

'How does all this fit in with that bank robbery at Wiggin Street?' Martin demanded. 'Is that what you're all arguing about, how to split up the money?'

'There is no money!' Packard shouted the words. They seemed to bounce back from the walls and echo round the small room.

'Then what are you fighting about? Why was Edwards after Georgina?'

'I've no idea!'

Martin sneered at him.

'You've no idea, yet you were hiding her in your flat? What did you do while she was there, talk about the weather and what was on the television? Or didn't you speak to her at all because you hadn't been properly introduced?'

Brady grinned. Packard looked from one to the other of them and when he spoke his voice was sullen.

'I asked her about it, but she wouldn't tell me.'

'Yet she expected you to hide her? You're not making sense.'

Packard pressed his lips together. His eyes were glittering and from time to time he glanced towards the door as if what he would have liked to do was spring though it and escape down the corridor. There was no chance of that, he knew; once the cops had their hooks into you there wasn't much you could do. He didn't know how they'd connected all this with the money, but if they'd done that, how many other facts did they have?

And did they know about Terry Stevenson and the fight in the scrapyard?

Did they know he'd been involved in that? Had they connected that up?

He sweated, not knowing and not daring to ask.

Martin, too, was worried. He was deliberately holding off sending someone to see if there was anything wrong at Hazel Manners' flat, knowing that the more worried about her Packard became, the more likely he was to crack. It was a risk, because there was always the chance that something might happen to her which he might have been able to prevent, but it was the quickest way he could think of to sort out the maze of lies and half truths which he knew Packard was feeding him.

'Who killed Georgina?' he rapped suddenly. 'Was it Mark Edwards?'

'It must have been. He was after her and he probably saw her going back home.'

'Why did he kill her?'

'I've told you, I don't know.'

'And if he killed Georgina, who killed him?' Martin paused. 'Was it you?'

'No.'

'Then if it wasn't you who was it? You've as good as said you were arguing with him. Did you kill him?'

'I didn't,' Packard gasped. 'I haven't seen him since yesterday afternoon.'

'That's when you were all together at his flat, is it?'

'That's right,' Packard said with a nod. 'We decided to get together and talk about it and — '

'Talk about what?' Martin asked as Packard's voice stopped abruptly.

There was a pause.

'I think you were all after the money,' Martin said softly. 'None of it's turned up yet, and that means there's fifty-five thousand pounds lying around somewhere. Did Georgina know where it was, and is that why she was killed?'

Packard hesitated. His mouth opened and closed twice. Sweat started out on his forehead, and there was absolute silence in the tiny room.

'The gang who pulled the bank job must have killed her,' he burst out. 'They wanted to stop her from telling me and Edwards what she knew. Edwards said she knew where the money was and that was why he was after her.'

'And you were going to join forces to get it? Where did Edwards go yesterday after he left you? If you can't tell me that it'll make you the last one to see him alive.'

Packard hesitated then he said: 'I can tell you where he said he was going, but I don't know whether or not he actually got there.'

'Where was that?'

'To see a bloke called Cummins, where Georgina used to work. He — '

'Cummins!' Brady exclaimed. 'The whispering wonder. I knew I'd heard that voice on the phone somewhere before. It was when I called Cummins' office yesterday.'

There was a silence and then Martin said tensely:

'If you're right and he's got Hazel we'd better get over to his place right away.'

18

'What do you think you're doing?' Hazel Manners cried.

'We're waiting for Lee Packard, my dear.' Cummins smiled at her, and the man with him give a faint twist of his lips. His name was Kilby, and there was something about him which reminded Hazel of a snake; he looked deadly, whether her eyes fell on the flat, hard expression on his face or the compact, chunky muscles of his arms or the way that he handled the gun he was holding.

He was the one who'd come to her flat.

As soon as she'd opened the door he'd poked the gun at her and there had been no escape, no alternative but to do as he said and go down the stairs with him. He'd had a car outside, with another man sitting in the back; they'd brought her here, and because of the gun it had been useless to struggle, even when they had hustled her out of the car, through a door

207

and along a passage with brown walls and no carpet, so that their feet clumped as they walked along it. The man with the gun had shouldered open a door at the far end and they came into what was obviously a hallway, with cream wallpaper and a grey carpet.

'Don't try anything cute,' he'd said, prodding her with the gun.

The other man had gone when Cummins had appeared, but there was still no point in trying anything cute. She had no idea what they wanted, though she knew they'd phoned Packard at least once because they'd asked her for his number.

'I'm just softening him up,' Cummins said. 'Playing on his nerves. By the time I've finished he'll be glad to come round here and listen to what I've got to say.'

'You've got that money, haven't you?' Hazel said, knowing that by revealing she'd guessed that she might be making things more trouble for herself but being unable to resist it.

Her eyes went to Kilby and his gun. She pictured him smashing that crowbar on to the head of that innocent passer-by at the bank, and there was no difficulty at all in visualizing it.

'I've got the money,' Cummins agreed. 'I've got you, I've got Edwards and I'll soon have your pal Packard. As soon as all three of you are out of the way the danger will be over for me.'

'You've got Edwards?' she asked.

'I had him,' Cummins corrected himself. 'He's dead now. His mistake was to come asking me questions about Georgina. I knew about him before that, of course, but I didn't realize until then just how close he was.'

'How did you know?'

'Fifty-five thousand pounds buys a lot of ears,' Cummins said vaguely. 'I get to know most things that are going on, one way and another.'

'I think you're talking too much,' Kilby said flatly. 'We should either get rid of her now, before Packard comes, or let her stew.'

Cummins shrugged.

'Does it matter?' he asked.

'Where did Georgina come into it?'

Hazel demanded, anxious to get them off the subject of whether or not to kill her. 'I know she used to work for you, but why murder her?'

'She found out too much about what I was doing,' Cummins said. 'When she realized that the business I run isn't entirely what it seems she thought it might be a good idea to go in for a bit of blackmail. She worked her way in through a couple of the lads I used on that Wiggin Street operation, but she was well out of her league and as soon as I went after her she ran. Edwards and Stevenson were after her too. It was inevitable one of us would get her in the end.'

'How did you come to find out that she was at Lee Packard's flat?'

'She phoned me, the little bitch, and said that if I didn't ease the pressure she was going to the cops. I arranged to meet her over at her place and talk about it.' He chuckled. 'Some dames never learn. She met me and I killed her. I think she thought she was safe because she'd told Packard some of the story and reckoned that he was a private detective who'd get her out of any trouble.'

'And you didn't think much of him?' Hazel asked.

'Not until the cops came talking to me about Georgina. They mentioned Packard's name and it struck me then that he might be a danger to me, so I sent a bloke to his rooms to see what I could find out.'

'It wasn't worth it,' Kilby said.

Cummins shook his head.

'But it was better than being left in the dark,' he said. 'Before he died, Edwards said that Packard got back early and surprised him.'

'We thought Edwards had sent him,' Hazel said, with a look at Kilby. 'I suppose you're going to kill both of us now, are you?'

'With fifty-five thousand quid at stake and clowns like you around, would you blame me?'

Hazel didn't answer that. She looked at Cummins, then at Kilby again, who was holding the gun so that there didn't seem any chance at all of surprising him.

'Packard will be running wherever I tell

him to by morning,' Cummins went on. 'He — '

A sharp ring at the doorbell cut him off. Kilby's eyes flickered towards Cummins and in that instant Hazel jumped up and tried to get the gun out of Kilby's waving hand. Cummins caught her a blow across the face which sent her staggering back, and she realized that she was a fool to stay here, struggling with them.

But somewhere in the house there was the missing fifty-five thousand pounds.

She hesitated, wondering what to do, and there was another ring at the bell, longer, and seeming more insistent than the first one.

That decided her. She didn't know why but she was certain this must be the police, and she turned, dashing out of the room. The money could be hidden anywhere in the house; there was no telling where it might be, and no time to look either. Even if she was wrong and the caller had nothing to do with the cops the best thing was to get out of the back door and see what was happening to Lee.

She ran to the door, her fingers scrabbling at the handle, then hurried along the passage where Kilby had brought her only a short time before. Her footsteps rang dully on the bare boards. Behind her there was a silence, though she wouldn't have been surprised to feel a slug smashing into her, or hear Cummins shouting.

There was nothing.

She reached the door and pulled it open, feeling the cool night air on her face as she ran out.

She ran straight into the policemen who were waiting there just in case anyone tried to get out that way.

* * *

'I think that's the lot,' Martin said, nearly an hour later. They were still at the house, and on a table in the room where the fight had taken place were two suitcases, both full of money. It hadn't been checked or counted yet, but to Martin it looked as though there was more or less the full amount.

'A pity about Hazel Manners,' Brady said.

'I don't think there's much we can charge her with,' Martin replied, 'though if what Packard told me is correct, she's a troublemaker.'

'A very smart troublemaker, staying on the sidelines like that,' Brady commented.

Martin nodded.

'If they'd all shot each other it would have saved us a lot of work. It seems as though Cummins' whole business was nothing more than a cover for things like that bank robbery, and if Georgina hadn't tried to blackmail him he'd have got away with it for a long time.'

He yawned. There wasn't much more clearing up. Kilby and Cummins had been charged, and Kilby, surprisingly, had already started to name the other members of the gang. Perhaps he was hoping that it would help him with the murder charge against him for killing that passer-by.

Packard was in a cell, charged with assaulting the policeman, Atkinson, whom he had punched in the stomach.

So far there were no other charges to hold him on, but that would give the police time to make full enquiries into his pickpocket activities, and the way Terry Stevenson had died.

'What happens now?' Brady said.

Martin gave him a surprised glance. It was nearly midnight, and getting very hot in the stuffy room.

'You can do what you want,' he said, 'but as soon as they come to pick up this money I'm going home.'

THE END

We do hope that you have enjoyed reading this large print book.

Did you know that all of our titles are available for purchase?

We publish a wide range of high quality large print books including:
Romances, Mysteries, Classics
General Fiction
Non Fiction and Westerns

Special interest titles available in large print are:
The Little Oxford Dictionary
Music Book, Song Book
Hymn Book, Service Book

Also available from us courtesy of Oxford University Press:
Young Readers' Dictionary
(large print edition)
Young Readers' Thesaurus
(large print edition)

For further information or a free brochure, please contact us at:
Ulverscroft Large Print Books Ltd.,
The Green, Bradgate Road, Anstey,
Leicester, LE7 7FU, England.
Tel: (00 44) **0116 236 4325**
Fax: (00 44) **0116 234 0205**

Other titles in the
Linford Mystery Library:

DEATH CALLED AT NIGHT

R. A. Bennett

Jimmy Ellis believes his parents have died in a car crash when as a young boy he is taken to live with relatives in Australia. The years pass happily, then the nightmare comes. Terrifying images flit through his mind in the dark — all through the eyes of a child, a witness to grisly events seventeen years before. He begins to delve into the past, and soon he finds himself on the trail of a double murderer — a murderer who is prepared to kill again.

THE DEAD TALE-TELLERS

John Newton Chance

Jonathan Blake always kept appointments. He had kept many, in all sorts of places, at all sorts of times, but never one like that one he kept in the house in the woods in the fading light of an October day. It seemed a perfect, peaceful place to visit and perhaps take tea and muffins round the fire. But at this appointment his footsteps dragged, for he knew that inside the house the men with whom he had that date were already dead . . .